THE AVARICE - A SEVEN DEADLY SINS ANTHOLOGY

Edited by

DAWN SHEA

This series is dedicated to Brad Tierney.
Thank you for the idea and the love and support you give the Indie horror community.

TABLE OF CONTENTS

THE SECRET RECIPE

NICO BELL

Sophie stood at her mother's gravestone with a heaviness weighing down her shoulders. It'd been six months since she'd been awoken by the ringing of her cell phone. The cop's voice held an air of detachment, as if he'd grown cold and tired from making those types of calls. He managed to get out a few pivotal facts—car accident, her mother, dead—before the rush of chaotic wails and tears overtook her. In that one moment, Sophie lost the only person in the world who loved her, believed in her, cheered her on when life got hard. They'd been a team, and now, she was alone.

Sophie turned away from the gravestone and walked back to her car. The gentle fall breeze wrapped around her as she navigated the landmine of graves until she arrived at the small parking lot next to the church. As she reached for her driver's door, the air chilled deeper and a coldness brushed against her cheek in a way that reminded her of her mother's reassuring touch—the same gentle sweeping of her fingers that dried tears when Sophie came home from elementary school crying because no one picked her for their dodgeball team; the familiar touch that brushed aside Sophie's long dark hair when Sophie hoped to hide the look of embarrassment on her face for not getting asked to prom.

She gasped and took a step back, looking around but seeing nothing except the evergreens lining the church's property.

"Mom?" The single word came out cracked and small. She frowned and shook her head, quickly getting into her car. Maybe she should pick up some Melatonin after work. Clearly, she needed more sleep.

Sophie drove down Main Street toward the small brick-front store that she and her mother had leased at the beginning of the year. Fresh tears threatened to surface as she pulled into the lot and stared up at the brand new "Grand Opening Soon" banner that hung in the window.

Babs's Bakery had been their dream. It started with Sophie's grandmother, Babs, who baked the moistest cakes in the county. The recipe became a guarded family secret passed down to Sophie's mom and, eventually, to herself. Babs won a few county baking contests, and Sophie's mom expanded on the notoriety by setting up a home business, but it was Sophie and her mom together that put all their savings into one lump sum and leased the brick and mortar. Between the bakery's start up and her mom's funeral, Sophie's bank account screamed for relief.

She walked up to the bakery's front door and took a deep breath. It'd be hard to do this without her mom. The grand opening was just a week away, and all their dreams—and Sophie's financials—hinged on making the bakery successful. Without the support, Sophie's stomach knotted as a seed of doubt sprouted.

Could she do this alone?

"Sophie?" A familiar voice called out from behind.

She turned and saw Mr. Williams, the property's owner, staring back at her. His bright eyes held a look of pity Sophie had grown accustomed to over the past months.

"Can we talk?"

"Of course." She unlocked the door and held it open for him.

The place still smelled like new paint.

"Can I get you anything? Coffee?"

"Um, no." He shifted from heel-to-heel. "I can't stay too long."

She noticed the way his eyes shifted and failed to meet her own. A tightness coiled in her chest. "Is everything okay?"

"I hate to do this, especially with everything you've been going through, but I was going over my records and it seems you've forgotten to pay last month's rent."

"Oh." Her mind tumbled around his words, trying to remember if she'd slipped the check into the mail or if the bill sat on her kitchen table amongst a pile of growing final notices.

"Of course, I completely understand how busy you've been." He held his hands up, palms toward her, as if surrendering. "I wouldn't even bring it up, except I need to pay the bank, and if they don't get their money—"

"No, it's fine. I get it." She plastered on a smile. "I'm sorry to put you in that situation. Do you think you could give me to the end of the week?"

"Sure." He turned and left Sophie standing alone in the middle of the room, her brain raking through the growing debt.

She sighed and ran her hands down her face. It looked like she'd have to borrow the money, and she knew the one person in her life who would have that type of cash on hand.

She groaned and pulled out a chair at the nearest table, sinking down, and preparing herself to call her mom's best friend Mandy. Mandy wasn't a terrible person. In fact, she'd been extremely supportive over the past months, not to mention a permanent fixture in her mom's life over the years which meant that Mandy had, in one way or another, been a big part of Sophie's life. The older woman lived an hour away, in the city, and spent most of her time building up a social media following as a fifty-year-old body positive woman, which Sophie admired. What she didn't admire were all the times Mandy flaunted her wealth. It made her and her mom feel like they were missing out on bigger and better life experiences.

And really, they were. Her mom died before getting to be successful, before they could reap the financial benefits of their business, before they could travel or try fancy restaurants or even get themselves better cars that didn't need constant repairs.

Still, Mandy had cash, and she'd said to call if anything was needed, and Sophie needed to pay rent on the bakery. She'd worry about paying Mandy back later. One problem at a time.

Sophie swiped at her phone and a second later, Mandy's smooth bright face appeared on her screen.

"I was just thinking about you!" Mandy beamed. "I wanted to take a drive out to visit and see how the bakery is coming along in preparation for the big opening."

"Actually, that's kinda why I'm calling." She looked around at the remaining items that still needed to be arranged and the few boxes that still needed to be sorted. It was coming together nicely, and if begging for rent money meant making her and her mom's dream a reality, so be it. "I need some help."

"Absolutely! Anything, you just name it."

"It's about our rent."

"Done." She waved her hand, flicking off the unasked question.

"But I haven't even—"

"Sophie, you know I thought of your mom as more than a friend. She was practically a sister to me, and I hope, over the years, you've come to think of me as family, the way I think of you as the same."

Sophie slouched her shoulders and gave a little nod.

"Good because family helps family, and I'm certainly happy to make sure Babs's Bakery gets off on a good foot."

"I'll pay you back as soon as I can."

"Sure, sure, if you insist."

"I'm serious." Sophie straightened her back. "It may take a little bit of time, but I promise I will."

"Actually," Mandy's voice held a bit of mischief. "I have a way you can repay me that works out for both of us."

Sophie forced herself to smile. "Oh?"

"This weekend I'm hosting a little baby shower for a friend. I was going to make cupcakes, but maybe if you could whip up one of your amazing cakes, we'll just call it even."

There were still plenty of things to do before the grand opening, but a cake was a much better deal than paying back rent money. "Okay, sure. Just text me all the details and I'll deliver it."

"Excellent. See you then!" She cut off the call.

"Sure." Sophie set her phone down and sighed.

IT TURNED out to be much more than a little baby shower. When Sophie dropped off the cake, half of the guests had already arrived. They swooned at Sophie's creation, a five-layer rubber duckie themed cake with adorable yellow buttercream details. Mandy's friends asked a million questions about the fine piping work, how much time it took, if she had a business they could link to on social media. They took pictures and decided on a hashtag before Sophie had a chance to catch her breath. She left after handing out all her business cards.

By the time she'd gotten back to the bakery, there was a text from Mandy.

Check out social media #BabsBakeryButtercremeBaby.

"Holy crap." Sophie sat in her car scrolling through her feed. People gushed over her sugary creation. They filled the comments with heart emojis and demanded to know where they could get their own. Mandy replied with the location of the bakery as well as a video of her tasting the cake.

"It's the best thing you'll ever eat," she said with a mouthful of icing.

A laugh bubbled up from Sophie's core as the comments filled up.

Can't wait to order my son's birthday cake!

I hear they'll be opening soon! I'm taking my kids to get cupcakes!

Anyone want to take a trip for the best cake ever?

Sophie smiled as warmth spread through her. "We did it, Mom."

She went to open the car door but gasped and quickly hit the lock button. A pale woman with blue-tinted lips stood outside of her driver's side door. The woman's mud-stained clothing hung limp from her frail frame and dark circles shadowed the woman's creamy eyes which bore directly through Sophie.

Sophie's scream filled the car. She fumbled through her purse for her phone, but just as her fingers gripped it, the cell slipped from her trembling grip.

"Shit." She looked away to pick it up and when she turned back toward the window, nothing but the familiar parking lot loomed outside.

Sweat beaded her brows as her pulse raced. She pressed her forehead against the glass, looking as far down as she could, but seeing nothing but pavement. The rear-view mirror reflected her own face, wide-eyed and mouth ajar. No spooky woman.

Her mind raced and replayed the moment at the graveyard, the cool breeze, the chilling feel that someone brushed her cheek. Her chest tightened and she squeezed her eyes shut, breathing deep, and holding for a moment before slowly releasing. The pulsating slowed and steadied until the tension eased and she opened her eyes, relieved to see that she was alone.

She forced herself to get out of the car and cross the lot.

There was too much work to do before the grand opening to worry about a random hallucination. Whatever she thought she was seeing was in her head, a result of too little sleep, her grief playing out.

Keep it together. Focus on what's real.

The new boost to her company was genuine and she needed to capitalize on it as quickly as possible. As her hands fumbled with the keys for the front door, her mind swarmed with the possibilities. Her mother imagined a small-town bakery serving their neighbors and friends, but what if this boosted their bakery to national fame? What if she could franchise?

A smile spread as her mind spiraled with the possibilities. It was wild to think anything would happen from one bump of positive social media, but what harm could it be to dream big? At the very least, she might be able to pay back Mandy sooner than imagined, as long as the acclaim translated to sales.

As she started to put away her purse and get comfortable for a long day of work, her phone rang. A bit of excitement replaced the earlier unrest as she went to answer, hoping it was someone calling to place an order.

"Hello?"

Static fizzled on the line.

Disappointment settled over her as the call dropped and the line went dead. It must have been someone in a bad reception area. She put her phone down and started the last of her prep work for the grand opening.

Soon, her life was going to change for the better.

THE GRAND OPENING turned into the type of spectacle Sophie and her mom dreamt of. A line snaked around the corner of the store. Sophie worked the counter alongside the small staff she'd hired when a woman with a child came to the counter. The woman looked familiar, but Sophie's mind struggled to connect the dots.

"What can I get you?" Sophie asked the little girl.

"One princess cupcake, please."

Sophie smiled and looked to the mom who gave a little nod.

"I don't know if you remember me, but I was at the baby shower your catered."

"Of course." Sophie smiled.

"I have to say, your cakes are incredible. If you don't mind me asking, what's your secret?"

Sophie chuckled. "Sorry, it's a family recipe. If I told, my grandmother would come out of the grave and shout at me."

"Of course. I get it."

The little girl was already licking the pink frosting off the top of the cupcake.

"I don't know if Mandy mentioned, but I'm actually a reporter for the city paper. I do a lot of small business profiles. If you have some spare time, I'd love to interview you and do a piece on Babs's Bakery."

"Really?" Sophie looked at the long line going out the door and wondered how much bigger she'd get with more positive press.

"Mandy mentioned that you started the business originally with your mother." Her voice lowered and her eyes softened. "I'm so sorry to hear what happened."

A twinge of anger sparked in Sophie's gut. Mandy shouldn't be telling strangers about her mom, but the anger quickly abated. Mandy was her mother's best friend. She probably told this woman as a way of grieving, of carrying on the memory, of working through her own pain.

"Yes," her voice cracked. "It was supposed to be the two of us."

"The article might be a nice way to share what you two worked so hard for." She reached into her purse and pulled out a business card, sliding it over along with payment for the cupcake. "If you're interested, please call me."

"Thanks." Sophie quickly slipped the card into her back pocket. She watched the woman and her daughter leave and quickly plastered on a smile as the next customer stepped up.

Her thoughts stayed on the conversation with the reporter as the day continued and slowed to a stop right before closing. She said good-bye to her staff and started closing up, alone and exhausted, but filled with excitement at what tomorrow would hold.

A news article had potential to catapult the business even further into success. Maybe another source would want to do a feature on her, maybe even a local television program would give her space to do a baking segment. Sales would flow in, and she'd never have to borrow money for rent again.

The clock on the wall said four in the afternoon. She didn't have much time to celebrate before she had to return and start baking again in order to fill her display case for the early morning crowd. Exhaustion battled with excitement, and a relaxing warmth settled in her chest.

Would her mom be proud? Of course. Everything they'd worked for was coming true.

She pulled out the business card and stared at it. As she reached for her cell phone, a knock on the door caused her to jump with surprise.

A young woman, about Sophie's age, stood on the other side of the glass door. Her dark eyes found Sophie's and held the stare.

"I'm sorry. We're closed." She gave a little wave and a smile and turned her back.

The knocking persisted.

Sophie frowned and again met the woman's gaze. "We're all out of baked goods. You'll have to come back tomorrow."

The woman didn't move. A hint of panic planted itself into Sophie. She clutched her phone and shook her head. "Please, you have to come back when we're open."

The woman reached into her purse, removed an index card, and slammed it against the glass.

Sophie took a small step back. Her pulse quickened. "If you don't leave, I'm going to call the cops."

Her words did little to deter the stranger who pointed to the card.

Sophie couldn't make out the scribbles. All she spotted were sloppy curves. The woman narrowed her eyes and curled her finger in a beckoning fashion.

"I'll call the cops." Her voice trembled. "I swear. I'll do it." She held up her phone, but the woman didn't budge.

The temperature in the room cooled and a chill shivered down her neck. The hairs on her arms stood as she looked around, but there was nothing except the familiar items of her bakery.

Again, the stranger knocked, but this time it was slow and patient, accompanied by her sly smile.

"Okay, okay." Sophie did her best to fake bravery. "I'll look at your stupid card, but then you have to leave, okay?"

She inched towards the glass, getting only as close as necessary. She squinted to make out the words.

¾ cup of white sugar

½ cup of butter

3 eggs

With each ingredient she read, her stomach knotted. Her throat dried and chest tightened. Sophie did her best to keep her tone steady but failed. "How did you get this?"

The stranger tucked the card back into her purse.

Anger flared in Sophie as her fists balled to her side. "How the hell did you get that?"

Her phone rang. Sophie jumped at the sound and cursed, keeping her attention on the woman who now wore a smug satisfied smile on her lips.

The ringing persisted, scratching at Sophie's nerves until she couldn't take it. She answered and shouted into the receiver.

"What?"

Static. Again.

"Shit." She ended the call and watched as the woman gave a little wave and started to walk away. Sophie's hand clutched the doorknob, ready to fling it open and demand this woman give answers, but she paused.

Somehow, this stranger got her hands on Babs's recipe, the one that had been passed down from one generation to the next, but what had she actually done? Nothing. She'd shown up, after the bakery closed, when all the customers were long gone, and done nothing. If she'd wanted to make a scene, she'd have done it while the grand opening was in full swing.

Sophie let go of the doorknob and watched the woman get into her car and drive away. Whoever the stranger was, she'd be back. Sophie was sure of it, but for now, she needed to think of a plan. She needed to make sure that her brand was secure whenever this woman decided to go public. If she decided to go public.

Sophie took a deep breath and dialed the reporter. It was time to set up that interview.

Sophie sat down at the table in the bakery across from Blake, the reporter. Two weeks had passed since the grand opening and business still flowed steadily. It'd take a while before she would actually break even from all of her investments, but she'd dipped into cash from the register to treat herself to a new dress for the big occasion. It wasn't everyday someone got to be interviewed for a feature position in the paper, and her picture would accompany the article. She knew her mom would want her to look her best. Blake set her phone down between them, the recording function on.

"So, let's start with the inspiration for Babs's Bakery."

"Well, my grandmother loved to bake. She was always in the kitchen making cupcakes for me and people in the neighborhood. My mom caught the baking passion and followed in my grandmother's footsteps, baking free birthday cakes for neighborhood children before starting a home business."

"That's so nice. Have you carried on that tradition? Baking free cakes for your neighbors?"

Sophie shifted in her seat. Honestly, she hadn't given much thought to the old practice. "Well, I'd like to, and maybe one day when the business has taken off, I will, but for now, I unfortunately have bills to pay."

She smoothed the wrinkles of her new dress as she spoke.

"Of course." Blake smiled. "Let's talk a bit about your cakes. You told me they're a secret family recipe."

"True. It's something that we've been working on for generations, and we finally perfected. They're the richest cakes in the county."

"So, what would you think if I told you that another woman has come forward claiming you stole the recipe from her?"

"What?"

Blake's perfect smile remained plastered on her face.

"I...I'd say she's lying."

"A woman named Abigail is on social media claiming she is actually the owner of the recipes you and your family have been using."

Sophie's mouth dropped open, but no words escaped. The

stranger. The woman with the recipe card. Sophie scolded herself for not getting ahead of the issue sooner, but everything happened so quickly. Now, she looked like a fool in front of Blake. The article, no doubt, would turn into a giant "gotcha" piece.

"Apparently, her grandmother worked for yours as a housekeeper. It seems that it's actually her grandma who used to bake cakes for the neighborhood children." Blake leaned a little closer, a hint of amusement in her eyes. "She's asking for you to admit that your family stole from hers and to either shut down the business or come up with a new recipe."

Sophie shook her head trying to wrap her brain around what was happening. She'd worked her ass off getting Babs's Bakery into existence. This wasn't just her dream. It was her family's legacy. There was no way Sophie was going to allow anyone to take it from her. Finally, she had something that was hers, a passion that made her money that would give her the life she and her mother had only dreamed of. No way was some random person who probably stole Babs's recipe—Sophie had no idea how that was possible, but clearly, it'd happened—and was using it to try and profit off Sophie's family's hard work.

Screw that.

"This woman is a liar. Plain and simple. Whatever recipe she thinks she has isn't real."

Blakes's eyebrows rose. "Would you stake your reputation on it?"

"I'll stake my entire family's reputation on it." She tipped her chin up just a tick.

"So, you'll accept the baking challenge?"

Sophie frowned and her stomach knotted. "What challenge?"

"She's challenging you to a bake off at the county fair next week to let the people decide if your recipes are the same."

A tiny warning went off in Sophie's mind, a little voice begging her not to do this. The recipe on the index card had been similar, at least the part she saw, but baking wasn't just about eggs and sugar. It took skill and finesse to combine them in just the right way, and that was something no one could steal.

Besides, this baking challenge would be another chance to showcase her bakery, another chance to bring in money and new customers. Maybe, with the profits, she could buy a new mixer for the bakery. The current one worked fine, but she'd had her eye on a shiny upgrade for months. Or maybe, she'd take all the cash from the increase in sales and put it towards the down payment for a new car. Or she'd break her lease and find a nicer apartment. Surely, she deserved to spend a little of her earnings to cheer herself up.

Besides, she was certain that she could beat this woman. Sophie was on the precipice of greatness, and that meant there would always be some jealous person trying to dethrone her. Sophie was up for the challenge. She'd destroy this woman while gaining more customers and soaring her baking empire into a new stratosphere.

NOW THAT SHE had the name of the mystery woman, it was easy for Sophie to track her down. A few clicks on social media, a couple online searches, and an address popped up. Abigail lived in a small house on the outskirts of the city. The roof sagged in the center and the paint peeled off the side of the building. Clearly, she needed cash.

Sophie frowned as she knocked on the door. It took a few moments, but the door swung open. Abigail answered with a surprised expression.

"We need to talk." Sophie didn't even wait for an invitation. She pushed past Abigail into the living room which was littered with take-out containers and dirty laundry. Sophie spun on her heels and folded her arms across her chest. "Where did you get that recipe?"

Abigail narrowed her eyes, and she squared her shoulders. "It belonged to my grandmother."

"Liar." She huffed and looked around the room. Dirt caked the windows allowing just a sliver of light to shine onto the pile of trash busting out of a small waste can. "You want money, right? Well, you're not getting a single penny."

The woman's back straightened. "I just want everyone to know that you're a fraud."

"My family didn't do anything!" Her heart pounded in her chest. She took a few seconds to steady herself before speaking again. "I know that your grandmother worked for mine, or at least, that's what you claim. If that's true, she clearly stole from my family."

Abigail huffed and shook her head. "It's the other way around. The only reason you're standing there with your shiny new company raking in money is because of my grandma. She was the one who worked her ass off getting that recipe perfect. Your grandmother stole it and paid her off."

Sophie snickered. "Well, clearly it wasn't enough."

"That's one thing we agree on." Abigail shook her head. "Your family built a reputation off that recipe. Eventually, that good name allowed you to open your store and profit, yeah? Well, it's time to pay up."

She huffed. "So, it is about money, just like I said."

"No." Abigail growled and took a step forward causing Sophie to backup. "My mom wanted to come forward, but my grandmother said it was best to let sleeping dogs lie. Well, they're both gone and buried, and I'm done being quiet. You took from us, and now, you're going to admit it in front of everyone, or else I'm going to win that bakeoff and prove that you're a fraud."

Sophie's anger brewed in her core. "Do you really think I'd let you take all of this away from me?"

Abigail smirked. "Do you really think I'd let you take from me?"

"I could sue you for defamation and slander."

"Do it. I'd love to make this even more public, and when you lose the case, I'll own your bakery."

Sophie's jaw tightened. "Bitch." She reached for one of the plastic forks that was sticking out of a food container. With it clenched in her hand, she lunged and stabbed Abigail in the eye.

Abigail screamed and stumbled backwards, hitting her back on the wall and sliding to the floor.

Sophie took an urgent step toward Abigail but stopped. She

stared down at the other woman who clutched her face as panicked curses flew out of her mouth.

"Call 9-1-1!" Abigail's hands felt around the carpet.

Sophie spotted the cell phone only a few feet away. She reached down and picked it up.

"Please, help me." Abigail panted as snot dripped down her face. "I won't say anything ever again. I'll drop out of the baking competition. I'll tell everyone I made it up."

"Where's the recipe?"

Her chest heaved as she whimpered. "It's on the kitchen table. Please. Take it. Just help me. I don't want to lose my eye."

A chilling sense of calm settled over Sophie as she watched the woman beg. "I can't risk it." Sophie picked up a lamp and slammed it over Abigail's head. Blood splattered the walls as she hit the woman again and again. The whimpers died until nothing but silence filled the room. Sophie dropped the lamp and moved to the kitchen where the recipe sat on a stack of old pizza boxes. She tucked the little index card into her pocket.

Eventually, someone in Abigail's life would realize something was wrong. Maybe before the bakeoff, maybe not. Someone would call the cops and they'd find Abigail in a bloody heap, but this was a rough part of town. Bad things happened all the time. Sophie took a steadying breath and left the house. Blood from her hands stained her steering wheel, but she'd clean it up later. No one would ever know.

APPARENTLY, no one found Abigail's body because the day of the bake-off came without any hiccups, which only confirmed Sophie's suspicion that the woman was a pathetic loser. Sophie packed up her supplies from the bakery and was getting into her car, eager to head to the county fair and claim victory.

A glossy eyed woman stood in front of Sophie's car with her head tipped to the side and a dark smile pulled across her face.

Sophie sucked in a breath as fear trickled into her chest. "What do you want?"

The woman didn't reply.

"Who are you?"

She thought she heard something—a whisper of a word—but the woman vanished before Sophie could know for sure. Sophie swallowed hard and hurried into the car, locking the doors the moment she slammed them shut.

The air chilled. Sophie looked up and standing next to her driver's side window was the same ghostly figure.

"No." She quickly started the car, looked in her review mirror, and screamed.

Another woman stood behind her car with similar milky eyes, but taller and with a toothless smile.

"Leave me alone!" She slammed the car into reverse and barreled backwards.

The woman vanished. Sophie slammed on the breaks. Her pulse raced and her chest tightened as another woman appeared in front of her car. Except, this one, Sophie recognized.

Abigail stood with dried blood staining the side of her face. Her eyes weren't glossy or pale, but black wells of rage focused solely on Sophie.

"This isn't happening." And then, they were in the car with her.

Sitting with her. Abigail sat in the passenger's seat, the others in the back. Abigail leaned forward, the scent of iron and rot filled the space between them, and she reached out her hand. Before Sophie could twist away, Abigail gripped Sophie's skull and squeezed.

"No! Stop!"

Sophie's mind was held hostage as images tumbled through.

It played out exactly as Abigail suggested. Sophie's grandmother taking a bite of cake, the cake that Abigail's grandma perfected. Abigail's grandmother swiftly being fired. The recipe masked as a family secret, passed to Sophie's mother, and soon to Sophie.

Abigail released and Sophie gasped. She managed to grip the car door's handle and open it, tumbling out of the car. With heavy feet, she raced back into the bakery as the ghosts looked on from the car. Quickly, she locked the door behind herself, a part of her refusing to believe the reality of the situation, but her eyes weren't lying. She watched them float out of the car, moving slowly toward the parking lot, until they stood outside the store's windows.

"I'll make it right." Sophie's voice cracked. "Please, let me fix it."

She ran to the cash register and opened it, grabbing the money with her trembling hands. She was about to throw it at them, but her hands refused to release. She couldn't. After everything, her body wouldn't let herself throw away all that beautiful cash. It was the key to her future. She tucked a few bills safely back into the register before hurrying back to the door. "This is what you want, right? Take it."

They just stared at her as she dropped the money and ran for refuge in the back of the bakery, away from the front door. She bolted into the storage room, but Abigail was waiting for her. Sophie yelped and spun around. Abigail's mom blocked the path back to the front of the bakery. Sophie bumped into a pot of boiled sugar that was still hot from earlier that morning, knocking it to the ground. It scorched her arm sending ripples of pain through her body. The grandmother materialized in front of Sophie and barred her rotten teeth. A small growl slipped through.

"I'm sorry." Sophie wept on the floor. The hot sugar pooled next to her. "Please. I didn't know. What do you want? What will it take to get you to leave me alone?"

The mother looked over at the flambe torch.

Sophie knew instantly what the ghost was thinking, but even in the midst of the terror, she couldn't, not after everything she'd been through.

Abigail appeared beside her and snarled.

Sophie whimpered. "I can't."

They're just ghost. They can't really hurt you.

The absurdity of the thought almost caused her to laugh, but the chuckle lodged in her throat when she saw Abigail pick up the torch.

"Don't." Sophie got to her feet. "I should never have hurt you. I'm so sorry, but I'll make it right. I'll tell everyone the truth. I'll bake the cakes and rename the place after your grandma, and I'll give the profits to anyone you want. Just please, let me keep this bakery."

But even as the words came out, Sophie knew it was too little too late. She'd let her own greed get in the way of doing the right thing and there was no turning back.

Abigail lit the torch and the flame danced to life.

The other ghosts moved toward Abigail with smiles on their faces. Sophie inched toward the back door but stopped.

Yes, she'd made mistakes, but why should she be punished because of drama her grandmother started? Anger welled up and she charged at Abigail. Sophie's body flung through the air as she lunged and slipped through the ghost, smacking her head against the oven door. She groaned as a splitting headache pulsated throughout her skull. Black dots floated around her peripheral as the ghosts gave her one final look before lighting the sugar. It burst up, the flames growing and catching the wall. Sophie tried to move, but the pain and confusion in that moment kept her rooted as warm tears slid down her face.

Smoke began to fill the bakery. The ghosts smiled as the room filled with heat.

Sophie's eyes burned as she watched them look down at her with a satisfied expression.

"I'm sorry." She managed a small whisper.

But she knew the truth. It didn't matter.

It was too late.

BALMINDER'S MIRACLE ELIXIR

JILL GIRARDI

December 31st, 2021
Eighteen minutes until Midnight

Jonathan Danvers pulled back the sleeve of his tuxedo and checked his Rolex for the tenth time that evening. Where in the bloody hell was Aralina? Still at the mansion with her bridesmaids, he guessed, stuffing herself into her skin-tight wedding gown and laughing at what a screw-up he was. Sure, it was true he'd been a screw-up, and a broke one at that, when he first met Aralina, but he'd sure hit the jackpot now. He'd come into an extreme amount of wealth and was marrying the girl of his dreams. No one could take that away from him.

At Midnight, his fiancé would approach on a path of rose petals, crossing the manicured lawn to the ornamental koi pond. There, they'd exchange nuptials in the first moments of the new year. Danvers thought it odd to marry at such a late hour, but he'd gone along with it at Aralina's insistence. He didn't want to argue with her anymore. Not the way they'd gone at it in the past. Tonight was a fresh beginning for the couple who'd navigated so many hardships in the last couple of years. They'd gotten through the worst of it, a period so mortifying they'd almost called it quits more than a few times. But they'd survived it, emerging from that dark tunnel with a love so strong even death couldn't break it.

A light breeze blew Danvers' salt-and-pepper hair over his eyes. The night air was pregnant with possibilities for their future as husband and wife. Living the good life on the sprawling estate in their luxurious mansion, traveling the world, free to spend their money like water if they so desired. Soon there'd be children. A little girl, button-nosed and sassy, with her mother's black locks flying behind her as she ran in the garden. Or a boy, tough and bull-headed, with Danvers' rugby players build.

At the thought of having children—vulnerable, sinless children—butterflies fluttered in the pit of his stomach. They were not so much the nerves of a groom at the altar as acute anxiety; an inexplicable feeling of impending doom. He wished Aralina hadn't insisted on holding the reception on the estate. If he looked hard enough, he could make out the family crypt in the distance. It was the place he'd interred his first wife, Edith, last March. It was distasteful, abhorrent even, to remarry in view of the vault where his first wife reposed. His bride-to-be chose the wedding location to remind him he'd spent twenty-five years with someone else. He'd taken too long to make her his wife.

Aralina had developed an obsession with his first wife, one that had escalated far beyond the realm of normal jealousy. She tortured herself with it, and she shared that suffering with Danvers in excruciating detail. She'd lay beside him in bed at night tormenting herself, asking him endless questions. How did you meet Edith? How long did you date? When did you start sleeping together? How did you propose? She pored over every photograph, fixated on every detail, and made herself sick with her endless need to know every aspect of their relationship.

Danvers had taken down the gigantic, somewhat gauche wedding painting that hung in the great hall and hidden it in the attic. But he knew Aralina sometimes climbed the stairs to gaze at the picture in the dimness, obsessing over every feature of his ex-wife's face. She'd made Edith far more important to herself than the woman had ever been to Danvers. He suspected his fiancé had read DuMaurier one too many times. It was almost as if she expected Edith to rise from her grave, moldy and vengeful, to take back what was hers. The very thought made him shudder with repulsion and more than a hint of guilt.

Because what nobody but Danvers and his fiancé knew was that Edith wasn't dead in the permanent sense of the word. She was only temporarily dead. That is, until he chose to revive her.

A photographer snapped candids of the guests guzzling the free-flowing champagne and loading up their plates, gobbling the hors d'oeuvres as fast as the caterers could replenish them. The sight of the delicacies such as goose liver pâté and caviar crème fraîche tartlets turned Danvers' stomach. He nibbled on a piece of avocado ricotta toast and nearly spat it out on the lawn. How could anyone eat such a vile fruit?

His late wife's family was old money and could trace their roots back to the seventeenth-century royal family. She'd tried to teach her husband—a former draughtsman from Leeds—the finer things in life, but he never took to the delicate and rather tasteless cuisine she forced him to eat. He still preferred his steak and Guinness to cuisses de grenouilles and Sauvignon blanc, but he was happy to inherit Edith's fortune upon her death. Or, rather, her almost death.

He circulated among the guests, his lips twisted in a tight smile. Let the freeloading vultures stuff their faces at his expense. He'd left Aralina in charge of the invitations—another big mistake on his part. Not having many close friends of his own, Danvers had told her she could handle it all—an idea she'd agreed to with tremendous enthusiasm. Now, thinking how she'd readily accepted the task, he couldn't be sure she hadn't planned it that way. Had she been coaxing him toward this the entire time?

She'd taken it upon herself to invite Edith's social circle. She was desperate to become a great lady, to rise in society, and have the same connections as the former Mrs. Danvers. Thus far, the women had ignored her to the point of rudeness, stubbornly loyal to Edith even after her untimely demise. The men showed a great deal of interest, mostly because Aralina was stunning, a beauty who could turn even the most snobbish of heads. Her gregarious nature and pretty, ready laugh was like honey during a famine, and she reveled in their attentions. This only served to further alienate her from the women, but Aralina simply tossed her head and continued flirting with their husbands, unaware she was thwarting her acceptance into the upper echelon.

Most of the other guests were friends of the vivacious young bride. They didn't like Danvers, but they came for the free food and the scandalous gossip. Her family refused to come, outraged at her choice of a widower twenty years her senior. Danvers was sure they'd change their minds after they'd reaped the benefits of his newfound wealth. He'd already inherited the mansion and the extensive estate property, and of course, all of the ready cash. Once the lawyers sold off the investments and released the funds to him, he'd be able to buy whatever and whomever he wanted. That included reluctant new family members. The gift of a new house or a vehicle thrown their way, and they'd accept him as if they'd chosen him for Aralina themselves.

He had few guests of his own, only his bosses and some colleagues, all whom Aralina saw fit to invite. His parents had died in India some fifteen years ago. Besides a sister in Sydney he hadn't spoken to in decades, he had no other family to represent him.

Danvers tossed the toast in the trash and continued moving through the crowd, passing by a woman in a satin dress more suitable for lining coffins than for her small frame. A little, round hat perched jauntily atop her head with a drooping feather on its crown. Danvers thought the feather made her look like a dejected parakeet. She was the wife of one of his bosses if he recalled. No matter, he was giving his notice after the honeymoon. He had money enough to live ten lifetimes, now. The only joy he'd gotten from working at C-TEK Fiber Optic was seeing Aralina every day, demurely sitting behind her desk outside his office. He loved the way she'd pretended to work, but in reality, was listening for any hint of him behind the wooden door that separated them.

"I can't believe he's getting married again so soon after his wife's sudden death," the bird-woman said in a bullhorn whisper. "For shame!"

"I knew Edith from Sunday Services," a woman in a red pantsuit replied. "A darling lady. Married beneath her station, if you ask me." Danvers didn't know who the woman was. A neighbor, perhaps someone from Edith's church, which he only attended on high holidays. He thought he vaguely remembered her face peering at him from over her horn-rimmed glasses. Edith was the one who'd kept up with that sort of thing. He'd never bothered to introduce himself to anyone. He'd often wandered off by himself at the endless stream of dinner parties and charity auctions she'd forced him to attend, chain-smoking Pall Malls and drinking himself into oblivion. He was aware they questioned why Edith, a socialite and former model, had chosen him above all others. He'd often wondered it himself. Perhaps, like Aralina, Edith had married him as a punishment.

"You know, she insisted he keep working after the wedding," the bird-woman continued. "She never gave him a dime while she lived. Oh, he enjoyed the good life—the clothes, the cars, the exotic vacations. But aside from the pittance of a salary my husband pays him, he never had any money in his own right."

"He sure has it now. And to think, he gets to spend it all on that cheap floozy he's marrying."

Grim-faced, Danvers pretended not to hear. He stalked to the far side of the koi pond and stood beneath a trellis festooned with white Arum lilies. Aralina had also insisted on that particular flower, and wouldn't back down no matter how he pleaded. She claimed the lilies were a symbol of their undying love and devotion, a rebirth, of sorts. Danvers now caught a lingering odor underneath the waxy aroma. It was the scent of death, of secret things rotting in hidden places. The same lilies had adorned Edith's coffin. Another penalty for failing to prove his love fast enough.

They weren't even married yet, and he already wanted to strangle his bride.

He patted the pocket of his trousers, feeling for the small vial he kept with him always. Three drops of the elixir inside had destroyed Edith; another drop on her cold lips would restore her. He planned to bring her back to life soon after the wedding, indeed, he'd meant to do it beforehand but he hadn't found the time to do so. She'd awaken without memory of the killing incident, could do nothing to prove foul play on her husband's part.

If Aralina wasn't careful, he might do the same to her. Also temporarily, of course. He could dead her for a while just to teach her a lesson. Not for more than a day or two, naturally.

He couldn't live without her that long.

January 1st, 2022
12:00 AM

The clock struck midnight, drawing Danvers out of his morbid reverie. The guests cheered, wishing each other Happy New Year. Raising their glasses high, they looked across the petal-strewn path with expectancy. The Marriage Officiate came to stand under the trellis, adjusting his collar and looking about him with a nervous smile. As per Aralina's instructions, the violinists began playing the song she had chosen for the wedding march: Auld Lang Syne. It was a strange choice even on New Year's Eve. Danvers felt a sour taste in his mouth as he thought of the words to the song. Another brutal reminder.

Should auld acquaintance be forgot and never brought to mind?

"Where's the moth-browed bride?" one of the guests shouted, causing the party to roar with laughter. Even the Officiate smiled with quiet benevolence.

The oblivious violinists continued to play their haunting

melody. A gust of wind blew a large number of the petals from off the pathway, leaving a bare spot in the grass and ruining the lovely scenery.

"Look!" the bird-woman shouted, pointing a ringed finger into the night. "She's coming from the opposite direction!"

All heads turned in the direction of the pointed finger. Danvers looked along with everyone else, but slower, the unexplainable feeling of dread returning. In the distance, the shimmery figure of a woman in white formed, hazy at first, then growing clearer. Why on earth had Aralina chosen to walk from the burial ground rather than the rose path? She had to circle around from the back of the house, the detour adding a good ten minutes to her wedding march. No wonder she was late. Danvers shook his head, annoyed, with a strange sense of foreboding, as if Aralina had done this on purpose, had planned the whole time to ruin the wedding just to get back at him.

He brushed the negative thoughts about his lover from his mind. She might be a little off her hinges, especially when it came to his former wife, but she loved Danvers as much as he loved her. That was why she did crazy things like this. She couldn't have planned to destroy their wedding ceremony. She would never do such a thing.

It seemed to take forever for her to arrive, a solitary figure with neither of her bridesmaids beside her. Danvers wondered why she'd chosen to make the march alone, and why the bridesmaids hadn't come down to join the wedding party instead.

The moon slid out from behind a cloud, casting its light on the bride at last and revealing the answers to all of Danvers' queries.

It wasn't Aralina who approached from the crypts.

It was someone—or something—else. Something green, and oozing, and wearing a Vera Wang wedding gown. Bone and muscle showed through patches in the rotting skin. A jawbone revealed itself through a gash in the cheek, glistening white. Instead of flowers, it clutched Aralina's severed head in her twisted fingers. The young woman's blood dripped from the shredded stem of her neck, staining the virgin white dress. The expression on the face of the disembodied head was one of extreme horror, agony, and pain. Danvers wanted to shut his eyes, to not see the look of suffering on his beloved's face, but he found he couldn't look away.

The wind stopped blowing. Paralyzed with shock and fear, the crowd stood in stunned silence, also unable to turn their heads from the gruesome sight coming nearer with every step. Even the crickets hidden in the grasses stopped their chirping when the creature appeared.

The thing in white raised the lifeless head in its bony arms and sent it hurtling into the lily pads in the center of the pool, like a bride throwing her bouquet to a group of flush-faced maidens. The fish shot away as it bobbed in the rippling water, their black and gold striped bodies flashing under the water. A red cloud of blood expanded on the brackish surface. Aralina's long, black hair came loose from the pearls that bound it as her head sank to the bottom of the pond.

The creature walked down the aisle, leaving a trail of foul-smelling slime in its wake, spilling blood on the pathway leading to the groom.

Now the guests shrieked like terrified Macaques as they scrambled to escape the fenced-in reception area. With bulging eyes and lowered heads, they stampeded toward their cars, giving the creature a wide berth as they tore past it. They fought and clawed, trampling the Officiate, his bones cracking under a dozen pairs of panicked feet, his face crushed to an unrecognizable bloody pulp. One of the violinists used his instrument as a weapon to beat his fellow musicians out of his path.

The bird-woman careened a bit too close to the creature, who snapped out a rotting arm and seized her by the throat. It bit down on her jugular, tearing the flesh from her neck. A ten-foot arterial spray shot into the night air, raining down on the terrified revelers. The feather in her hat came loose and fluttered to the ground.

The thing threw the bird-woman aside, her body bouncing as it hit the grass. It focused its dead eyes on the groom, who stood paralyzed under the trellis. It was then that Danvers realized who it was —or would be—if not for a single malicious act on his part.

It was his deceased wife.

Edith.

AUGUST 31ST, 2020

"YOU PROMISED she'd be dead before the end of the year." Aralina slid into the warm water of the hotel swimming pool in her new string bikini. "There's only four months left, Johnny."

She pooched out her lips, pouting the same way she did in her Instagram photos. Danvers thought she looked rather like a horse stretching its lips around a lump of sugar. Still, he found Aralina's long, toothy face irresistible, even when she was nagging him to kill his wife.

They'd snuck down to the empty pool to fool around for a while. Danvers' existence had long ago grown stale. The allure of these illicit weekends got him through his days. Aralina was his salvation. He'd hoped to enjoy this last night with her before he returned to his mundane life as a manager at C-TEK.

But much like his wife's still-beating heart, his girlfriend just wouldn't quit.

"I'm turning thirty next year. My late father would be heartbroken if he knew his daughter was still single at such an age." She sighed with dramatic abandon, pulling off his shorts to give him an underwater tuggie. "Oh Johnny, I'm so in love with you. I can't bear the thought of sharing you with another woman."

Danvers moaned with pleasure. He felt he'd do anything for her —even kill for her—when she touched him like that. He ran a hand through his silvery hair and tried to distract her with a kiss. She pulled her hand away and dog-paddled in front of him, looking at him with disgust.

"No more lovemaking until we're married."

"Lovemaking?" the older man scoffed, hurt by her rebuff. He'd always thought their trysts were more bestial than devotional. "Don't start getting moral on me now, darling. Not when you want me to murder Edith."

Aralina's big brown eyes widened, her mouth contorting into an expression of pure fury. "I've been sleeping with you for two years, and what have you given me in return? You think I'm some kind of whore?"

Danvers let out a hoarse, unpleasant laugh, interrupting her tirade.

"How about all the things I gave you today: a Coach bag, a year's supply of Mac cosmetics, and multiple orgasms. That, my dear, makes you a whore by its very definition."

His cheek stung from the slap she gave him before she splashed her way to the ladder and climbed out of the pool.

"Anyway, I faked all those orgasms. You can't even get it up without a case of Viagra!"

Infuriated, Danvers was about to reply with more scathing remarks when security came. By then his shorts had floated to the center of the pool. He covered his genitals with his hands and swam out to retrieve them. Aralina hadn't even blushed. She just stood there laughing at him, her bronzed body wet and glistening in the moonlight.

There were no poolside towels at that late hour. They'd had to ride the elevator, swimsuits dripping wet, while the other occupants gawked at them. Danvers kept his head down while Aralina glared back in proud defiance. Back in the room, she toweled herself off, dressed, and grabbed her new Coach bag from the floor. Carrying it to the black lacquered dresser, she held it open like a gaping mouth. Tubes of makeup clacked together as she swatted them into the bag. Then she was gone, slamming the door behind her.

Despondent, Danvers went to bed and lay awake for an hour. He was bankrupting himself for this woman, even stealing money from his wife, yet his lover showed no appreciation at all.

He got up and went over to the large windows overlooking the pool. As he gazed outward, he realized anyone looking out of the windows would have seen it all. No wonder the security guards had smirked while throwing them out of the pool area. As much as he hated the tempestuous battles they waged at least twice a month, Danvers loved Aralina. He wanted nothing more than to spend the rest of his life with her, as toxic as that might seem to the rest of the world.

He picked up his cell phone and called her several times, but she didn't answer. He felt he couldn't stay alone in the room a minute longer. He grabbed his wallet and keys and stormed out of the hotel.

Once outside, Danvers crossed the street to the busy promenade. It was a muggy night, and although it was late, locals and tourists alike were out in full force. Some young girls sat on the tan-colored brick wall overlooking the sea. Their fresh, pretty faces and easy laughter reminded him of Aralina. It made him even more depressed.

He sat on one of the cement benches that lined the sidewalk and took out his cell phone, playing a casino game to distract himself from his troubles. As he was playing the slots, a dark shape appeared in front of him. Danvers looked up to see a tall, handsome Sikh man, dressed in black, with a black turban wound around his head. The man peered down at him with a puzzled frown on his bearded face.

"What do you want?" Danvers growled, assuming the man was going to ask for money. He set his phone down on the bench, close to his thigh so no one could snatch it.

The big man put his hands out. "I am a fortune-teller..."

"Not interested." Danvers turned away, considering the conversation finished, but the psychic wasn't ready to give up.

"Sir, you are having a crisis of the spirit. I want to ease your pain."

"How the hell…" Danvers shouted. A few tourists looked over at him. He lowered his voice to a whisper. "How did you know that?"

"Your aura called out to me as I passed. Please, may I sit?"

With his mouth agape, Danvers moved over on the bench to make room. The fortune-teller sank down, his face shifting into a smile, exposing his long, white teeth. To Danvers, the Sikh's dark, hooded eyes seemed to hold an ancient knowledge in their depths.

"Have you made up your mind to do this then?" the psychic asked in a grave voice.

Danvers knew what he meant. He wasn't even surprised the man had divined his secret.

"I don't want to do it." It was a relief to admit this. Edith wasn't a bad woman. Still… "It's the only solution."

"You can divorce your wife, or run away with the girl. No one has to die."

He thought of all the debt he'd incurred, the funds he'd stolen from his wife. The finances he'd need in the future to keep Aralina happy.

"I need the money!"

"Then it is not love that drives you, but greed."

There was no sense in denying it, not to this man who could read the signs of the universe.

"Tell me what to do!"

The mystic sighed. "I can only advise you on the right path to follow. The final decision must be your own."

"Get out of here!" Danvers shouted, his face growing hot with rage. "You're a scam artist looking to make a quick buck."

When the psychic didn't move, Danvers jumped from the bench, raising his fist in the air.

"I said, get away from me!"

The fortune-teller rose, in no rush despite the threat. At his full height, he appeared enormous beside the older man. He gave Danvers a long, cryptic glare, then turned his head to eye the cell phone on the bench. He waved his hand over the device and mumbled some obscure words in Punjabi. He turned back to Danvers.

"Go ahead and play your game now. It will solve all your troubles."

"W-what?" Danvers stammered.

"Technology is the Savior of the Unsaveable, the Righter of Wrongs, The Evener of the Uneven," the fortune-teller said. He gave an inexplicable little bow and walked away down the promenade. He soon disappeared into the crowd.

Danvers' shoulders sagged. He'd managed to evade a fight with a grizzly bear. He defied the curious stares of the crowd by picking up his phone. The casino app had frozen. He restarted it and began playing the slots with gusto.

After a few minutes, the game paused itself. A video ad began to load.

The screen was black at first, but soon a figure began to materialize in the center. Danvers sat up straight, stifling the cry that welled up in his throat. It was the Sikh fortune-teller. Of that, Danvers had no doubt. He had the same piercing dark eyes and full black beard. His shoulders were double the width of an ordinary man.

"Are you in despair, Jonathan Danvers?" The mystic asked in his guttural voice. "Are you forced to make an irreversible decision?

The mystic disappeared from the screen. An animated scene loaded. Danvers watched himself return home after a long day at C-TEK. He saw himself removing his coat as Edith entered the room. She was sipping from a coffee mug and clutching a fistful of papers, which she thrust in her husband's face. Edith was accusing him of having an affair, of siphoning funds from her bank accounts. She threatened to leave him, to write him out of her will. Danvers stammered, unable to deny the accusations.

Then his hands were around Edith's throat. Spirited classical music played as he squeezed tighter. Edith sputtered and gasped, her face turning purple. She clawed at Danvers' hands, which had somehow turned into fat, white-gloved paws. A laugh track played as he rocked her back and forth, her head swelling to ten times its natural size. When he released her, Edith's head deflated as she whizzed all over the room like a popped balloon. She landed at her husband's feet.

Then he was bending over her, checking her pulse. He howled and tore at his shirt, shook his fists at the ceiling, gnashed his teeth. He threw himself over Edith's flattened body and wept.

The front door flew open with a crash, and the mystic entered to the cheers of an unseen audience. Danvers looked up, his face bewildered and pitiful.

The mystic held out his hand, revealing a dark glass bottle small enough to fit in his palm.

"Everything would have been fine," he exclaimed as he grinned at the camera, "if you'd only used Balminder's Miracle Elixir!"

The fortune-teller snapped his fingers, and the scene began to rewind itself. It started again when Danvers arrived home, this time coming in through the back door. He went into the kitchen and took the mystic's glass vial from his pocket. Opening it, he shook three drops of liquid into the coffee pot on the counter. Then Danvers exited the back door. Moments later, he re-entered through the front of the house. The sitcom started over.

Edith came into the room, again holding her mug and those damning documents. She took a sip of coffee before launching into her tirade. Suddenly she froze, her face turning various shades of green before she dropped to the floor in violent convulsions. Within minutes, she'd expired in front of Danvers' Florsheim Wingtips. He never even had to touch her.

"Watch what happens now!" cried the fortune-teller.

He took yet another vial from the folds of his clothes. Leaning over Edith, he applied a single drop to her unmoving lips. At once, the woman rose, hale and healthy, unaware she'd been dead only seconds before. Appearing confused, she wandered out of the room without acknowledging her husband. Nor did she address the black-garbed giant who stood nearby.

The screen faded to black, and the mystic reappeared in unanimated form.

"Murder your wife and inherit her riches!" he shouted, his deep voice thundering with enthusiasm. "No police involvement as there's no actual crime committed. No evidence of foul play after autopsy. That's our guarantee. One hundred percent satisfaction or your money back. Click the link below to order."

Stunned, real-life Danvers tapped the link before the ad could disappear. The website began loading, and a line of text flashed across the screen. It vanished before he could read the entire message. It was something about resurrecting the body within three hundred days or…

Or what?

Danvers quickly forgot the disclaimer. Those were only for precaution anyway, insurance against unforeseen liabilities. This was the solution to all his problems. For the first time in months, he felt a glimmer of hope forming deep in his marrow. It wouldn't be murder if he brought Edith back to life. He'd inherit her money and marry Aralina. With that much wealth pending, a man could hire a lawyer who'd speed through the probate process. By the time Edith returned, he'd have legal ownership of everything. She'd have no claim to her money or even to him. There was no precedent of a dead wife coming back to strip her heirs of their fortune.

Oh, he'd see to it that she lived the rest of her life in comfort, of course. And who could protest if a grief-stricken widower took a young bride to console him in his grief?

He added one bottle of the miracle elixir to his virtual shopping cart and checked out using his debit card. He paid an extra fee for express postage and used his office address for the shipping.

The phone rang. It was Aralina calling. He'd let it ring for a minute before he answered.

Danvers smiled to himself. Soon, he would have everything he'd ever wanted.

January 1st, 2022

Just after Midnight…

. . .

DANVERS MANAGED to break free of his paralysis just as Edith reached him, his heart pounding so hard he thought it might be the onset of a heart attack. The thing grinned hideously, ripping the threads of her sewn lips. Pools of blackened blood spilled from the corners of her mouth. The stench of her foul breath overpowered the scent of the flowers around her. Her long arms reached for her husband. He grabbed the side of the trellis, and with a mighty heave, pushed it on top of the hideous creature. She fell beneath the weight of the wood. Pinned beneath it, she hissed and struggled to free herself. Danvers made a mad dash for the mansion, screaming as he raced forward in blind terror. As he went through the doors, he dared to look over his shoulder.

Edith had already thrown off the trellis. She got to her feet, tottering on heels not made for the dead to walk in. At least, the cumbersome shoes slowed her down.

The lawn was complete chaos, with drunken partygoers fleeing in a dementia of horror. The staff had abandoned ship at first sight of the rotted bride, with security close on their heels. They rushed from the estate grounds, spilling onto the street packed with New Years' celebrants. Danvers sprinted into the house, looking for his fiancé. He darted up the spiral staircase toward the suite of rooms he now shared with Aralina.

He had the elixir in his pocket, but how could he restore Edith now? She would tear him to pieces before he even touched the potion to her lips. And who knew if the juice would work on her now. His only hope was to contact the mystic. He alone would know how to stop the creature that even now stalked Danvers on spindly legs.

When he reached the suite, he saw the door was ajar, propped open by Aralina's headless corpse. She was wearing her wedding dress, one Danvers now realized was a copy of Edith's burial gown —another sign of her jealous obsession with his first wife. Blood pooled out, staining the plush carpeting. Danvers let out a wail and fell to his knees beside his beloved's corpse, holding her headless body in his arms.

"Oh, baby, no!" His bride-to-be was dead, and it was his fault. Something had gone terribly wrong. The elixir hadn't worked as advertised. He remembered the disclaimer he hadn't bothered to read. Something about restoring the victim within three hundred days. Was this what became of the corpse if one failed to heed the instructions—the rapid decay of a body once preserved? How long had it been anyway? He frantically tried to calculate the date.

Much to Aralina's dismay, he'd held onto the bottle for several months, too afraid to give his wife the killing dose. When had he finally gotten up the guts to use it? March 6th, after a colleague's birthday party, he remembered. Danvers counted the days since then. 299, 300, 301.

The elixir had expired yesterday.

And at the stroke of Midnight, his dead wife rose.

He'd been so wrapped up in Aralina's diabolic wedding plans and endless meetings with lawyers. He hadn't realized the date of expiry had passed.

If he survived, he was going to leave the mystic one hell of a bad Yelp review.

Down the hall, the door that led to the stairwell flew open. Danvers caught sight of the bloody burial gown. Edith had made it upstairs and was coming toward him, step by dragging step. With a cry, Danvers grabbed Aralina's arms and pulled her into the hall, leaving a trail of blood on the carpet.

He ran into the suite, slamming the door behind him. In the sitting room, he found the bodies of Aralina's two best friends, torn to pieces. They'd been helping the bride with her hair and make-up. Now their corpses lay masticated beyond recognition, even their faces chewed to a bloody mess. Danvers vomited, the front of his tux stained with Moët & Chandon and his fiancé's blood.

He'd left his cell phone in the bedroom when he went down to the reception. Now he ran into the room and grabbed it off the mattress. His hands shook so much that he dropped the phone twice. He opened his contacts list and tapped the hotline number for the mystic's website.

"Sorry, the number you have reached is not in service."

"Fuck!" Danvers screamed. He called again and got the same message.

Now Edith was banging on the door. What would she do to him if she got him? He imagined her tearing him to shreds with her manicured fingernails, his flesh coming away in ragged, bloodied strips.

Danvers opened his browser and found his bookmarks. He clicked the link titled BALMINDER'S MIRACLE ELIXIR. The connection was slow. He waited in agony for the site to load.

FIX_ERR

THIS SITE CAN NOT BE REACHED.

ERR_ADDRESS_UNREACHABLE

DANVERS FELL TO THE FLOOR, his body jerking with the violence of his sobs. The mystic was forever out of reach. Edith would have her revenge.

"It's 2022," he moaned. "Humankind can put Wi-Fi hotspots in outer space and has plans to colonize Mars, but hasn't found a way to stop internet scams."

He heard a soft, almost inaudible click and knew Edith was inside the sitting room.

Danvers dug in the pocket of his trousers, looking for the little vial that had caused so much trouble. He pulled it out, unscrewed the cap, and swallowed three drops of the dark liquid. Next, he grabbed a sheet of monogrammed stationery and a Montblanc pen from the roll-top desk in the corner. He scrawled instructions for whoever found his body, offering a substantial reward to anyone who revived him within three hundred days. He set the bottle of elixir on the bed, along with the note.

He hoped he'd be dead before Edith reached the bedroom.

GREEDY PIG

LYNDSEY ELLIS HOLLOWAY

Where the fuck are you?

I'm at African drumming with mum, remember? It's Wednesday.

Spending more fucking money, again.

Matt, I'm not spending money. Mum pays for the sessions for both of us so that I can come. She just wants to spend time with me,

You never think about me, do you? It's all about you. You get to go out drumming with your mum, you get to spend money on stupid shit, while I sit here and wait around for you. Why can't you use your brain for once in your life and think about me?

He put the phone down on the arm of the sofa and smirked as it vibrated like a nest of angry wasps. She hated it when he didn't respond to her, especially when she knew he was pissed off with her. He watched the phone buzz away, shuffling along the arm of the sofa as it continued its irritable dance as she attempted to call him, before finally falling silent. Like he'd have fucking answered, he didn't have the energy to listen to her half-arsed excuses as to why she'd gone drumming with her mum again. Maybe a night of silence would finally get it through her thick skull that she was *his* and he was done sharing her time with other people.

Matt sneered at the phone as he got up, abandoning it in the living room as he went into their bedroom. He fucking hated this house, it wasn't remotely up to his standard of living, but he was working to rectify that. He'd grown tired of going back and forth to pick up his useless girlfriend from her dead-end job as a general assistant for a supermarket. It had taken a while for Lucy to understand that she was meant to be there for *him,* that *he* was the most important thing in her world and that *she* should have been making sacrifices to make him happy. Eventually, he'd got through to her that she needed to do better, and once he'd pushed her to apply for jobs in the hospital alongside him. The pay was better and it meant he could keep an eye on her, her time was his after all and now they could see each other during the day and at home as well. Just as it should be.

He sat at Lucy's dressing table and tapped a finger on the lid of the jewelry box she kept there, opening it to reveal the meager contents. Most of it was shitty costume jewelry, sentimental shit her equally useless family had bought her for birthdays and Christmas presents. Nothing of any real value, then again what could he expect from them? They were pathetic. Yet there was some potential, not a lot, but a little. He grinned at the ring, pride of place in one of the central trays of the jewelry box and he plucked the glistening band out, turning it around in between his thumb and forefinger.

The gold band, with its setting of diamonds and rubies, was simple but stunning in its own way. Lucy never wore it, it was too small for her fat fingers, and she'd never bothered to get it resized. If she was waiting for him to do it for her or thinking he would get her a ring, she'd have to buck up her ideas first. When she'd been working one Saturday at the supermarket—leaving him alone all day, bored and without anything to do—he'd taken the ring and got it valued out of interest. She wasn't worth anything else, whatever she owned of value *he'd* bought her, except for this. Her great-grandmother's ring was worth far more than Lucy probably knew, and he intended to make sure she sold it when the time was right.

It wouldn't take much. He'd managed to persuade her to stop wearing her childish t-shirts and wear more suitable clothing when around him. He had no intention of walking around with her on his arm when she looked like some teenager that hadn't grown out of cartoons. No, she wore more appropriate clothes now, she looked half-decent anyway, though he still had a lot of work to do with her.

The ring would get him the house and the dream car that he wanted. She owed him that after all the crap he put up with from her. He'd spent two years running her back and forth to that dead-end job of hers since she couldn't drive. Even now he had to be her personal chauffeur because she'd never bothered to spend the time learning, which meant *he* had to risk his precious car getting scratched by idiots that didn't know how to drive. She knew how stressful he found it, but she didn't do anything to help him out. Ever. They wouldn't have the house they lived in now if he hadn't sold his precious car to get them the deposit to rent. She owed him for everything she had, and she *still* left him to spend money on frivolous things like coffees and lunches with her mum.

He hated her mother. She was an interfering know-it-all who hadn't realized that her daughter had outgrown her, that Lucy was *his* now and she should just back off. He'd managed to weed out the morons Lucy had called 'friends', over time, and now none of them would talk to her. Her family, on the other hand, were proving to be more difficult to get rid of.

Her mother seemed determined to undermine him at every turn, vying for her daughter's attention and trying to encourage Lucy to do things on her own, to branch out without him. What Rebecca hadn't understood, yet, was that Matt was the one in power in this relationship. Not Rebecca, not Lucy, Matt. He knew what he wanted, he knew what was due him, and regardless of that absurd woman's ideas, she wasn't going to win against him.

Lucy *loved* him, she *needed* him. That was plainly obvious to anyone that saw the way she begged and clung to him if he ever threatened to leave her. He wouldn't, of course, she was perfectly pliable and useful for what he needed. She needed him, she wanted his approval and she was so easy to manipulate. It wouldn't take much to coax her down the path he needed, he'd managed to get her to cancel several plans with her mother before now, and he knew that this would be the last time he discussed this 'drumming' nonsense with her. She wouldn't *dare* defy him over it again, not this time, not after the silence.

He heard a car door shut and smiled as he put the ring back in the jewelry box, shutting the lid and striding out of the bedroom, back to the living room. He lingered by the window, hidden behind their blackout curtains as he listened to his girlfriend saying good-night to her mother.

"So I'll pick you up from work next week then?" He heard Rebecca say, that hint of hope in her voice made him smile, clearly Lucy had already begun to sow the seeds to her mother that this was the last time.

"I-I'll see, mum, it depends on how tired I am after work. OK?" Lucy replied hesitantly, and Matt scowled.

She'd always hated confrontation, but she managed to shout back at him when she felt the need, so why couldn't she step up and see that *he* was her priority? She needed to be home for him, not galavanting with her mother over stupid shit like this. Her mother didn't need her anymore, Matt wanted her home and she was going to *be* at home.

"Oh. Alright then." Her mother replied softly, but there was no hiding the disappointment.

Matt smiled again, his heart pounding in his chest with this renewed victory. Lucy hadn't quite said no to her mother, not outright, but Rebecca knew that pushing the issue was a lost cause. Her daughter wouldn't be coming to drumming next week, or the week after, or ever again. Not now Matt had hold of her.

"Well. We love you, maybe we'll see you over the weekend? The both of you?" Rebecca added hastily.

Matt snorted, sneering as he continued to eavesdrop on the conversation. No, not if he could help it. He'd allowed Lucy to see her family every other week, but he'd already started to wean her away from them, finding reasons (or forcing Lucy to make them up) as to why they couldn't see them. This weekend would be no different. He wanted to look at houses, and he was aiming to have her pawn her ring if he could push the right buttons to make her do it. He just had to keep at her, as he had before, and then he would have everything that was due him.

"I'll let you know. Love you mum." Lucy replied, her voice hitched in her throat.

His lip curled in disgust at the tone, she was pathetic. Everything she did annoyed him, but she would be better once he shaped her to his liking. She was malleable, which was rare at the best of times, and it would take some work, but he could make her what he needed. She gave him power, she didn't fight him, and whatever he needed she would give him. In the end. That little sob sticking in the back of her throat was the last act of defiance from her and he wouldn't continue to tolerate it. Once and for all Lucy was going to come to the realization that her place in this world was dictated by Matt and his wants and needs, not hers. Not anymore.

He heard her utter another goodbye to her mother as the car pulled away and he sat down on the sofa, shoving his phone into his pocket as he turned the TV onto football. Brow furrowed, arms crossed over his chest, he stared hard at the screen and waited for the inevitable shuffling from his meek spouse. The front door shut quietly and he listened intently as she moved around in the hallway, putting away her coat and shoes just like he'd taught her, rather than just kicking them off and leaving crap lying around on the floor as she'd done in the past. Finally, he heard her take a deep breath, shuddering and barely able to hold back the inevitable tears as she dared to open the living room door.

"I'm home." She muttered under her breath, not quite daring to speak louder than a whisper.

Matt didn't say anything in return, instead, he picked up the TV remote and made a point of turning the volume up as though to drown out her very existence. He was skilled at this, not that she was difficult to manipulate at the best of times, but all the power was in his hands and she was helpless, unable to do anything to counter him.

"Matt please." She begged, already sobbing.

"Fuck off." He snapped, his eyes still on the television, not that he had to look at her, he knew exactly what she looked like.

"Matt. Please, just talk to me! I was just drumming with mum, you know she likes to do things together, it's one night a week and I'm not even paying for it, she is!" Lucy added frantically.

Inwardly Matt smiled, whenever she got this defensive and desperate it was because she had already lost. He'd learnt that a couple of years ago with her, as though this was her last-ditch effort at regaining some sort of power within their relationship. She was so naive. She had no power here, not over him, not even her tears could sway him. If anything her crying just made him more determined, didn't she *ever* realize how she affected him with her selfish actions?

"I said fuck *off*." He snarled again, throwing the TV remote in her direction without looking away from the TV.

He heard her yelp and felt a tiny blip of satisfaction that he'd managed to hit her with it. She never took the time to understand his feelings or think about how leaving him alone on an evening once a week might make him feel. Why did she think it was OK to go off and have fun without him? If she loved him surely she'd want to do these things *with* him, wouldn't she? Wasn't that how this worked?

"No, I won't." She whimpered, moving in front of the television to force him to look at her.

He scowled at her, keeping his amusement hidden within as he saw her rubbing at her arm where the remote had clearly hit her. Good. He hoped it hurt. "You were the one who left me all fucking night. So don't come crying to me like I should care, or have sympathy for you. Why do you think I give a shit about you, when you clearly don't give a shit about me?"

"I *do*!" She wailed, dropping to her knees.

He whipped his hands out of her reach, sneering in disgust as though she was some foul creature that had dared to touch him.

Instead, she clung to his legs, resting her head on his knee as she wept.

"I love you, why can't you see that? I'd do anything for you." She whimpered into his leg, her voice muffled against his jeans.

"Oh fuck off. Stop lying to me, I fucking hate lying cunts like you. You don't love me, if you did you would never have gone out without me. Don't you get that? I would *never* do anything like this to you, leaving you all alone on an evening after work when all you want to do is relax with the person that's meant to love you. But that's because I'm not selfish, unlike *some* people."

He heard her sharp intake of breath and couldn't help the smile that crept onto his lips. She was too easy, so much so that this wasn't even hard anymore. A little bit more and he could have her doing whatever he wanted, she would finally be all his. No more texting other people, no more seeing her family, she would be at his beck and call at every hour of the day.

"I'm sorry, I'm so, so sorry." She wept. "I'll quit drumming, I won't go anymore, I promise."

"It's not *just* about the fucking drumming. How fucking thick are you?!" He snarled, rapping his knuckles hard against her head as if to knock some sense into her physically. "The drumming is just *one* thing, but it'll be something else. You'll find another excuse to go off without me with your mum, or your dad, or something. You don't love me at all."

"I do! I'm sorry Matt, just tell me how I can prove it to you, just tell me how I can show you how much you mean to me. I'll do anything, anything at all." She insisted, looking up at him, her eyes bloodshot as she clung to his jeans.

There. There it was. That final piece, that last little bit of confidence and defiance gone, shattered in the wake of his anger and disappointment at her. Her parents could say nothing now, whatever they said to her, she would ignore, she was his, at last, all his. Just as she should be.

"You really want to prove to me that you love me?" He asked

slowly, watching to see if there would be any further argument on her behalf.

"Of course I do, just tell me what to do." She begged.

"Alright. You message your mother and tell her you no longer want to see her or any of your family. This weekend we're going to go look at houses, you need to find a second job to help pay for the deposit and the mortgage, I'm sick of fucking carrying you, it's time you paid me back what I'm due. I want you to sell anything of value, like I did my car, that way we can speed things along and *finally* have a house of our own, where we can be together like we're supposed to be." He stated simply, watching her to see what her reaction to this would be.

"But… Matt I." She gasped, her eyes wide as she processed what he'd just asked her to do, she looked as though she wanted to be sick. Of course, the cutting ties to her family would be the most difficult thing to ensure she did, but he was determined, and there was no way she was going to defy him this time.

"What? I thought you said you wanted to prove to me that you love me." He snarled.

"I do. I'll do it. But I don't have anything of value to sell." She muttered, sitting back and staring up at him in disbelief.

She put her hand on her chest and he smirked, wondering if her heart had finally broken. She couldn't deny him a damned thing, he was in charge here and if she wanted to spend time with him, and be with him, then she would do exactly what he wanted.

"You do. Your great-grandmother's ring." He said simply.

She fell back, her hands barely stopping her from collapsing in shock at his suggestion. He'd never met her grandmother, and he wouldn't have cared to even if she'd been alive when they'd met. All he knew was that the ring was worth something, and it was going to be his.

"Matt… I can't." She whispered, barely able to get the words out as she stared at him.

"Oh, so it's ok for me to sell my car, and downgrade and be expected to pay for everything but not you? It just sits in your jewelry box and does nothing, you don't even wear it. If you loved me, you'd sell it so we could get a house, but clearly, you don't want the same things as I do." He reiterated.

"I-I do, Matt, I do. I'll… I'll go into town Saturday while you're with your dad and sell it to a jeweler." She muttered, head down, shoulders slumped in dejection as she finally gave in to him.

"I want to see a receipt as well, make sure you're not stealing money from our future. If I'm still going to have to drive you around everywhere, the least you can do is take the burden off me money-wise. And think of some way to make some extra money, Avon or something, I'm sick of being the only one who pays for anything in this house. Now, let's go to bed." He demanded, standing up and stepping around Lucy without offering to help her up.

He heard her scramble to her feet behind him and he grinned. Finally, everything was falling into place. Soon he would have his house, his car, and all the money he could want once she was working two jobs. He'd have to push her to do better at the hospital and get promoted, but it wouldn't take much, not when she was so desperate for his approval.

"How many fucking times do I have to repeat myself?!" Matt snapped, slamming the car door behind him as he got out, glaring at Lucy over the new vehicle's roof. "Surely you understand plain fucking English?!"

"I said I was sorry, Matt!" Lucy wept in response, hurrying from the car to follow him into their new house.

"I don't give a shit about your excuses anymore, fucking sort yourself out. Make me my dinner and just shut the fuck up, for once in your life. And don't make me something shit, make an effort this time." He added, heading straight into the bedroom and slamming the door behind him.

Matt threw himself onto the bed with a smile as he heard Lucy clattering around in the kitchen, soft sobs echoed from the kitchen as she clearly attempted to fight back her tears, to no avail.

Lucy had told him she'd agreed to dinner and drinks with her colleagues a week from Friday. Apparently, she hadn't quite understood him when he'd said she wasn't to socialize with other people. He wanted all of her time, he wanted her all to himself, she was his, and that was the end of it.

He passed the time playing his football games in the bedroom until Lucy dared to knock on the door to let him know dinner was ready. They ate in silence, the meal was decent for once, not that he was going to tell her that, she needed to be punished for continuing to defy him after all before they finally went to bed.

Matt groaned as he woke the next morning, his entire body ached, his head groggy, as though he'd spent the night before drinking heavily. Sitting up slowly, he glanced at Lucy's side of the bed, glad to see that she was up and out already, making him his coffee and breakfast as he expected her to. Blinking he raised a hand to rub the sleep from his eyes, wincing as his skin pulled and stung on his right arm. He stared at his arm in horror. A large patch of skin on his forearm was inflamed and red, glistening with a sickly white film as the skin around it almost bubbled. He tentatively reached to touch it and hissed at the feeling of his fingers against the exposed nerves, as though he'd just poured acid over the wound rather than just touching it.

"Lucy!" He roared, throwing the bed covers from his legs and grimacing as any movement caused the exposed skin to pull. "Lucy!"

He heard her footsteps thunder down the hall as she ran from the kitchen, throwing open the bedroom door to see what was wrong. Matt pointed to his arm, unable to form any words as she hurried over to inspect it. Her hand reached out for his arm, and Matt whipped it away, wincing at the movement and inwardly cursing himself for it since his entire arm was now on fire.

"What happened?" Lucy asked.

"How the fuck would I know? I woke up like this!" He snarled.

"I think you'd better see a doctor," Lucy muttered. "I'll call them now, you can't go to work like this."

"At last, she finally uses her fucking brain." He growled, watching as she picked up her phone and called the doctors. "You'll have to fucking drive."

"Matt..." Lucy whispered.

"I can't like this, can I? Use your fucking head."

Lucy nodded, ducking away to talk to the doctor.

Matt stared at his arm, the skin glistening in the sunlight as he attempted to get dressed with one arm. He had no idea what had happened, but the sight of the skin, blistering and peeling at the edges, angry red in the center, made him feel nauseous. He closed his eyes and swallowed hard.

"They want us to go to A&E," Lucy spoke softly, dragging Matt back from his thoughts.

"Alright, let's go." He snarled.

Lucy managed to drive them to the hospital without incident, though there were a couple of times when Matt ended up snapping at her because she got too close to another car. Though what could he expect from her really? They sat in the waiting room and waited for their turn, the skin tingling whenever someone moved past them, causing the air to shift and brush against it, making it sting all over again.

"Matthew Thompson?" A doctor finally called, looking around the room and offering a smile when Lucy waved a hand to indicate where they were sitting. "Follow me please." The woman smiled.

Matt followed the doctor into a private room, Lucy lingered by the door while he sat on the edge of the bed, holding his arm up for the doctor to take a good look at the problem.

"I have to ask, did you spill some oil on your arm while cooking?" The doctor asked, looking at Matt seriously.

"No. I woke up like this. Lucy does the cooking at home." Matt replied sharply, irritated that the woman clearly hadn't listened to a word he'd said about why they were there.

The doctor looked at him, then at Lucy who smiled weakly at

her, catching Matt's eye before she looked away sheepishly under his stern gaze.

"Well. I'm not sure what's caused it but we can clean it and dress it, just keep an eye on it and if it gets any worse come back. I honestly couldn't tell you what brought it on. I would swear it's from hot oil." She sighed.

Hot oil. The words ran around and around Matt's head when they finally left the hospital. How the hell had he got this wound in his sleep, especially a wound that looked like it had been because of an oil burn?! He stared at Lucy as she drove them back home, staring straight ahead as she concentrated hard on the drive. If he'd thought she had it in her, he'd have suspected Lucy, except she was too weak to do anything so daring and surely he'd have woken up if she'd dared to do anything that vicious. No, it wasn't her, but whatever it was... he just hoped this was the only one.

"I've got to go to work. Will you be alright without me?" Lucy asked.

"I'll have to be, won't I, since you're leaving me here," Matt growled.

"Matt... I can't just... I... do you want me to call in sick?" She finally relented.

"Do whatever the hell you want." He replied dismissively, shutting the bedroom door and leaving her in the hallway.

Matt lay on the bed, staring at the dressing on his arm, his mind still turning over what the doctor had said. How had he even *got* the wound? It didn't make any sense. He looked around the room, searching for anything that might have fallen from the ceiling or something, but there was no evidence of *anything* that could have caused the wound. The door opened and Matt turned over, unwilling to look at Lucy as she shuffled into the room.

"I brought you something to eat, you need to keep your strength up." She muttered.

Matt snarled under his breath, turning slightly so that he could look over his shoulder and glared at his other half. He watched her put a tray down on her dressing table, laden with a cup of tea and a bowl of rice and chicken. She'd never been overly inventive when it came to food, but at least for once, she'd made him something he didn't mind.

"I'm going to get you fish and chips for tea, OK?" She added. "If you need anything, just call for me."

"Like you can do anything for me. You know what, why don't you just go to fucking work, you're no use to me at all." He snapped.

"I love you." She whimpered, hurrying back out of the room, closing the door behind her.

Matt rolled his eyes and got off the bed, shoveling the food down his throat and washing it down with the cup of tea before he lay back on the bed. His arm was numb from the mild anesthetic the doctor gave to him, but the rest of his body still tingled with the memory of that hot pain lancing through his arm right into the bone of his shoulder, making his fingers feel like they were going to explode. He grimaced and rolled his shoulder, staring at the door as though he expected Lucy to come back. He blinked, his eyes heavy. When had he become so tired? He'd been fine a minute ago. Another blink, this one longer this time, and he felt his head droop on the pillow, his body like a lead weight on the bed.

WHY DID the whole world seem to ache? Matt groaned, furrowing his brow as he pinched the bridge of his nose, focusing on that rather than the fact that he felt like he was on the sea. Matt's stomach rolled and he gritted his teeth together, swallowing hard against the nausea that washed over him.

"Lucy?" He groaned, reaching to her side of the bed with a hand, his jaw aching as he continued to grit his teeth when his arm reminded him of its wound, the anesthetic had worn off while he slept.

The bed was empty, she'd got up as she usually did. Or was it just later in the day? How long *had* he been asleep? Matt took it slowly, opening his eyes a little bit at a time until he got used to the lighting in the bedroom. He stared at the ceiling for a minute, eyes focused on the lampshade above his head as his stomach decided to backflip with his head. Once he'd settled, he dared to try and sit up, crying out as his arm twinged and pain rocketed up his left leg.

With his good arm, Matt threw off the bedsheets, or at least he tried to. He screamed, gripping his leg just above the knee as though that might somehow stop the spread of agony now radiating from his toes to his hips and beyond. White-hot, it felt like someone was peeling his skin one layer at a time. The duvet had moved when he'd thrown it, but the sheet beneath was stuck to his leg. The white material was sticky and red with a sickly yellow tinge around the edge that finally made Matt vomit. He leant over the side of the bed and wretched, screaming through each convulsion as he put pressure on the wounded leg.

"Matt?! Matt what's wrong!" Lucy screamed, running into the room, the door slamming against the wall in her haste.

He heard her gasp, but it barely registered, all he could think about was his leg.

"I'm going to call an ambulance, don't move!" Lucy screamed.

Slowly, Matt sat up, wiping the spit and vomit from his mouth, staring at the red patch on the sheet that covered the wound on his leg. He wanted it off, he wanted it *off*. Gripping the edge of the bed with one hand, he took hold of the sheet with the other and pulled, as if pulling a waxing strip from his leg. The soft sound of skin tearing from his leg and a renewed flash of pain made him vomit again and he trembled as he stared in horror at the huge, wet blister that covered his entire calf. Much like his arm, the flesh was red with a shiny white film over it, but above that had formed a huge yellow bubble that leaked fluid slowly onto the mattress beneath.

"What the hell is happening to me?!" Matt screamed.

He stared at his reflection in the dressing table mirror, his eyes wide, his face pale and gaunt. He barely noticed when Lucy came back into the room, lingering in the doorway with her phone in her hand, staring at him.

. . .

No one could work out what caused the first two wounds, nor any of the wounds that followed. Matt was in and out of hospital almost daily with a fresh wound, his skin pockmarked with blisters and red-raw flesh. The doctors had taken swabs, but the results didn't show anything conclusive and no one could quite understand *where* the blisters and burns were coming from. The only thing anyone could attribute them to was hot oil burns, but no one could understand how he'd got them.

The hospital had tried to commit him, to keep him under observation, but Matt refused, he wanted to stay home, he worked in the hospital, and the last thing he wanted was to bloody stay there. The doctors hadn't been pleased, but at Lucy's insistence, they'd agreed, leaving her instructions on how to clean and dress his wounds so that he didn't get infected, and demanding that they have regular updates.

Lucy had given up her job to take care of Matt full time, unable to juggle his schedule around work. She'd sold his car, his *dream* car, to make ends meet, and now they were having to sell their house. His *dream* house.

"I've got the movers coming in an hour, so I need to get you to the new house before they arrive. Here. You need to eat your lunch and take your medicine before we get you into the car." Lucy whispered.

He glared at her, taking the tray from her and watching her as she taped up the last of the moving boxes. She looked haggard, all the light had gone from her eyes and she'd stopped making the effort to do up her hair and makeup. Every minute of her day was spent taking care of him, but if she *really* loved him, she'd have found a way to keep the house and the car until he recovered.

Every movement was agony, the bandages that covered his numerous wounds restricted him and pulled on one another. His last round of medication was wearing off, and he was starting to *feel* the patches where his skin had slid off entirely, leaving fresh raw skin and exposed nerves screaming at the world. The pain was in his bones now, every inch of him hurt and just *being* was painful.

Matt spooned the soup into his mouth, swallowing carefully, hoping not to make anything else hurt as he did so. Once he was finished, Lucy took the bowl away from him, handed him a glass of water and his pills, and then helped him to the car. The seatbelt pressed uncomfortably against his bandaged chest, and Lucy did what she could to relieve it, but there was only so much that *could* be done.

"I'll just get some of the boxes we can take, I'll be two minutes." She whispered.

He didn't care. He watched her go back into the house and sighed heavily. Once he was better, he would get his house back, and his car. She would just have to work harder, that was all, clearly, he hadn't gotten rid of all her distractions or they wouldn't have been in this mess at all. Matt rested his head against the window, glad of the cool glass against his forehead. His eyelids began to droop and he scowled. Why? Why was it that he felt tired every time he ate something? He blinked longer than he meant to, and when he opened his eyes again he saw Lucy's face outside of the car window, grinning at him. She looked wild, a mixture of the Cheshire cat and Hannibal Lector rolled into one. Panic swept the pain away and he tried to reach for his seatbelt, but his hands refused to move. Matt felt his eyelids begin to close again and he wanted to scream, but no sound came out, and he was left with the image of Lucy grinning insanely at him as he fell asleep.

MATT WOKE WITH A START, his first instinct was to scream his girlfriend's name, since he could still see her wild eyes staring at him, but no sound came from his mouth. The second he tried to cry out, something bit into his tongue, eliciting another attempt to scream from him and only making the situation worse. The more he tried to say anything, the more it seemed to clamp its sharp teeth onto his tongue. He coughed and spluttered, blood filling his mouth and spilling from his lips along with a river of saliva. His jaw ached, but it was just one new pain amongst several.

His entire head was encased by something metal, the plates pressed against his skin, cutting into his mouth and preventing him from speaking. He tried to reach up to touch it, but his arms couldn't move either, but the second he jostled them he felt his shoulders scream in protest. His chest labored, his vision blurred and his head felt like it was in a washing machine as he tilted his head as best he could in the strange metal contraption, staring up in horror at his arms held above his head. He quickly looked down and realized that he was at least on the ground rather than suspended, but that offered little to no comfort with his hands restrained above him on a pulley. He stared around him, trying to work out where the hell he was; it was dark and empty, the ground was a mixture of concrete, dust and debris from whatever had been here before. It was a warehouse, but that was about all he could discern from what he could see.

"Ah! You're awake! I thought I'd given you too high a dose this time." Lucy's voice echoed around him in the empty space.

Matt tried to turn to face her, but the ropes dug into his wrists and elicited another scream and another wave of blood.

"Oh, I really wouldn't make any noises. The scold's bridle really isn't forgiving, after all, it was meant to stop women from speaking. Ironic really, if we'd met each other back when they were used, you'd have made me wear one, wouldn't you?" She laughed, walking into view at last.

He recognised her, and yet he didn't. She held herself with confidence he thought he'd broken, her hair brushed out of her face, clean of any makeup. She wore one of those infuriating 'geek' t-shirts of hers from the Alien franchise that he was sure he'd made her get rid of. And her voice… there was a sultry tone to it, tinging the malice and joy in each word that slipped from her tongue.

"You wanted all my attention, didn't you? You wanted me to be with you *all the time*. I cut out my friends, I gave up my interests, and I told my family I no longer wanted to see them. I changed jobs, in fact, I got *three* jobs just to keep you happy. But it was never enough, was it? I dealt with you putting me down and beating me, but you just wanted more and more. The final straw? Was the ring. You got greedy, asking me to pawn it. Oh I know, I did what you asked and I sold my ring as you told me to, and we bought the house and the car you wanted, but it still wasn't enough even after you took everything from me."

Lucy sighed as she took hold of Matt's waist, and smiled at him. It wasn't an expression he recognised on his girlfriend, she'd never looked so wicked and content as she did now. His heart pounded in his chest and he was sure she would be able to hear it. Matt whimpered, staring at her in desperation, hoping she would come to her senses. He couldn't speak, he couldn't ask her to let him go, it even hurt to breathe in through his mouth, forcing him to breathe through his nose. He gagged on the stagnant air, but there was something else, something thick and cloying and filled with a hint of smoke. Something he recognised but couldn't quite put his finger on. He coughed and winced, every part of his body begging him to stop moving.

"Ah, you've smelled my little surprise," Lucy whispered, kissing him on the cheek. "Before I show it to you though, I wanted to assure you that *no one* is going to find you, or in fact give a shit about what happened to you. I wasn't the only one you hurt over the years, Matt, I wasn't the only person you took everything from, was I? Did you think I wouldn't find out about the others? About the women who came before me? You cast them aside when you were done taking everything from them, but you saw more potential in me, didn't you? You're a greedy fucking pig, Matt, always wanting more from everyone but never willing to do anything yourself. You just devour people, using them to get what you want. Well, it doesn't matter now, because I found them, the girls from before me, and they helped me to get you here." Lucy giggled, her hand covering her mouth as she pretended to be coy, and that's when he saw it.

Even in the dim light, the rubies and diamonds *gleamed* upon her finger, his eyes fixed on it. Lucy saw where he was looking and laughed, holding it up in front of his face.

"Oh yes, I sold your precious fucking car and bought my ring back. Hannah was *more* than happy to keep it to one side for me once she heard it was *you* that told me to pawn it. That's when she reached out to the others, and they helped me plan it all out. I suppose I'd better show you my surprise now." She grinned.

Matt stared at her as Lucy stepped out of his field of vision, straining against the ropes as he attempted to follow where she went but he couldn't. Suddenly the warehouse flooded with bright lights, and Matt closed his eyes against the glare, grimacing. He heard the mechanical whirring of gears and screamed, the sound cut short as the scold's bridle bit into his tongue mercilessly, his arms were pulled higher and his feet left the ground. The weight of his body, suspended from the rope around his wrists, made his pulse race as his brain tried to understand that pain coursing through every inch of him.

The rope juddered and moved him from where he'd been standing, slowly taking him along a pulley system attached to the ceiling until it came to a sudden halt, causing him to swing back and forth. Tears blurred his vision as he tried hard not to make any sound, his chin wet with blood and saliva, his head hanging limply on his neck as his entire body shook. When he came back to his senses, close to blacking out with the pain, he began to panic again.

It was hot beneath his face, and that cloying smell was now thick and suffocating, coating his nose and making his skin feel greasy as he desperately tried to breathe through it. Through the thick steam and light smoke, he saw a huge metal cauldron, a fire roaring beneath it, causing the sickly yellow liquid inside to bubble.

"Do you know what the punishment for Greed is in Hell, Matt? I didn't, until I started researching the Sins, you see I wondered what sin I committed to be stuck with you. I don't think I did anything, until now anyway, I suppose now I'd be Wrathful. I can look forward to being dismembered alive, but you? You, well, you get to be boiled in oil!" Lucy laughed gleefully. "I took my time… I made sure the sedatives that Grace gave me worked, and I isolated you just like you isolated me. I gave you *exactly* what you wanted, all of me, and now I'm going to take all of you. Slowly, but surely, I'm going to lower you into this vat of boiling oil and I'm going to listen to you scream, just like you listened to me scream." She whispered.

Matt's heart stopped, his pulse grew quiet and everything went numb. When he felt the rope begin to descend he came back to his senses and screamed, the bite of the scold's bridle forgotten as he writhed back and forth against his restraints, desperate to escape what awaited him. A high pitched squeal filled his ears, and it took him a second to realize that *he* was the one making it, his feet felt cold but that too took a minute before it registered with his brain that it wasn't cold at all - it was white-hot.

Inch by inch, Lucy lowered him into the vat of oil. He felt his skin blister and burst, watching in horror as his girlfriend stood and watched his skin peel from his bones. Behind her, as if to rub salt in his wounds, Matt's final vision before the pain stole his consciousness, were the women that had come before Lucy, standing beside her grinning as the oil consumed him.

All seven of them.

QUOTA

RUTHANN JAGGE

LEANING BACK in her oversized plush chair, Marlena Bliss nervously twists her long blonde hair back into a loose braid, then pivots to look at the computer screens surrounding her on three sides. At a glance, she can determine sales and profit on every platform used to market the exclusive products she represents. Candy wrappers, stained teacups, and half-empty water bottles clutter her stylish mid-century desk. She hasn't left her office in days. Marlena's breaks from her work are short naps on a nearby couch, listening to the sounds of the ocean surrounding her upscale apartment located near a pristine beach. She seldom gets to enjoy her surroundings. She's always working. Panic sets in, and she turns toward an open window, trying to catch a whiff of the fresh salty air outside. She unconsciously nods, agreeing with the column of numbers displayed in front of her. My highest sales week ever. Marlena's head drops onto her hands, resting them in front of her on the desk. She knocks a gold-rimmed teacup to the floor, flinching as it shatters. She is terrified.

The young woman struggles to breathe, sucking in stale air through her expensively veneered, perfect white teeth. She can taste her achievement, but her office also reeks of nervous sweat.

Marlena is relieved and determined to maintain her ranking at the top of the performance chart for the month. Her elite standing as "Premier Seller" will be shared with all of the teams via email by the President of the "Deliciously You" company himself, Raphael "Rafe" Bernal. But her impressive sales numbers will also mean another increase in her quota.

Rafe's profile photo on the "Deliciously You" website makes her want to lick the screen. He's dark and brooding with an unruly swatch of hair swept back into an elaborate Viking knot at the crown, shaved close on the sides. His blue eyes flash sparks. Rafe has the look of a model on the cover of a romance novel. The company's promotional videos that Marlena has on repeat in the background show his love of outdoor adventure, motorcycles, and fast cars. In her favorite one, he's wearing a tuxedo, with a topcoat draped over his shoulders, caressing a sizeable purple jar of cream like a lover. There's a large silver ring with a skull, tarnished to fashionable perfection, on his hand. His predatory look is incredibly seductive.

Several weeks ago, Marlena was browsing pages of limited available job listings while considering an upload of her shoebox of naughty photos, taken during a drunken romp with an ex, to an unsavory website promising good pay. She's desperate for a reliable income. A tinkling sound on her social media page with a mediocre follower status alerted her to a private message in her inbox. Gaining attention in a sea of flawless and accomplished people has proved next to impossible for the average-looking young woman, despite her consistent but amateur efforts to become an "influencer." She doesn't offer anything exceptional and can't attract the attention necessary to profit from her efforts.

"Hello, Marlena.

We've noticed your fabulous style and think you'd be a perfect candidate to sell our luxury line of organic personal care products. We only consider truly unique people to represent our brand. We're eager to connect and discuss your future with "Deliciously You" at your earliest convenience. The link below is nontransferable and will expire in twenty-four hours, so please reply soon.

We look forward to a long and successful adventure together.

Deliciously Yours,

Rafe"

Marlena couldn't believe her good fortune. She is swimming in debt, and despite recently completing a community college degree, it isn't enough to land a job worthy of her time and effort, let alone one with a livable salary. Her options become more limited by the day. Tapping the screen impatiently, she quickly researches the company, clicking through dozens of links featuring photos of lovely people enjoying life to the fullest. There are hundreds of glowing reviews and verified customer comments praising the high-priced, elegantly packaged line of "Deliciously You" products. Each item is organic and proprietary and is a limited edition, which increases the demand even further. The prices are high but include free shipping. These exclusive products have fabulous results when used as directed and cumulatively on the faces and bodies of the brand's discerning clients. Photos of satisfied buyers, all gorgeous people with radiant skin, toned bodies, and flowing hair, validate the company's claims. The profit percentages and bonus rewards "Deliciously You" offers as incentives are not only appealing, they're amazing.

The offer to be involved with such an elite business is thrilling. Without hesitation, Marlena responds via the limited-time link, then fills out an extensive and invasive questionnaire requesting personal information. She ignores the intrusion and only hopes she's approved as a consultant. The young woman is eager to begin selling online right away. Within minutes, a congratulatory email arrives, assuring Marlena that she is among the few the company considers worthy of representing them as a sales consultant. Details are transferred, including graphs and brightly colored pie charts defining her potential for an impressive salary and commissions and a few specific financial conditions one must meet for an initial inventory. She agrees with them all, initialing on every open space.

Another email arrives. The "Deliciously You" logo is written in an elegant purple script at the top, with tracking information for an overnight shipment. A weekly supply of products is on the way to her shabby studio apartment. She must use them all, taking photos and notes on her results to share with others interested in purchasing the lotions, cleansers, and creams. Marlena needs to experience the impressive effects firsthand for training purposes. The email generates from a staff member's desk named "DeeDee." They promise Marlena will be ready to begin selling as quickly as possible. One starred detail at the bottom of the list mentions there may be "other costs and expectations involved for her supply at a later date," but Marlena chooses to ignore the footnote, brushing it off as something to deal with if or when it happens.

Eager to get started, Marlena forces herself to make a judgment call out of her moral comfort zone. Her resources are limited, as is her income, and minimum upfront payment is due as a condition of hire. She uses her deceased grandmother's social security number and information to apply for a loan online, securing several thousand dollars she doesn't have in minutes.

Investing in a supply of inventory produced by the "Deliciously You" company is mandatory, so she quickly decides to commit fraud. Her car needs better tires, and she hasn't had a meal besides cheap fast-food specials in weeks, but Marlena considers potential and future more of a priority. Her parents named her after the deceased woman she has no memory of, so it's an easy process, and a slight twinge of guilt does not deter Marlena. No one has ever given her a dime or a second thought, and she's struggled since leaving her family home at age eighteen. Marlena wants a future as bright as the smiles on the faces in the photos elevating the glorious company's image.

A few clicks later, funds transfer to the "Deliciously You" International Holdings account, and a musical tribute confirms that Marlena is now an "authorized vendor of the world's most coveted beauty brand." Wholesale costs for her weekly products will be deducted from her monthly earnings before any balance hits her account. A company debit card will allow reliable access to her funds. She spends some time browsing the enticing website created just for her, boasting her name in a glamorous stylized font at the top. The professionally designed site bursts with how-to videos, before and after examples showcasing remarkable transformations and dazzling product close-ups. There are subtle links to purchase each item with a single click, with all sales credits automatically added to her newly established portal. In her excitement, she didn't consider how quickly the entire process came together.

A random photo of Marlena, supplied upon request, is prominently displayed on the homepage. The young woman is gloriously filtered and lit to perfection. Marlena gasps at the unnatural representation of herself but loves how marvelous she looks, prompting her to set new goals for herself to ensure her manipulated image becomes her reality. There's also a password-protected page that only she can access, with a monthly "expected sales" quota based on her growth and reach as an official brand influencer, her monthly earnings, and any deductions for her products, with wholesale pricing, of course. Marlena's eyebrows raise at the amount listed as the "minimum sales acceptable" for her first month. She's somewhat uncomfortable with the number of zeros. Influencing will be a full-time job for the foreseeable future.

Her social media platforms have been automatically polished and updated with her new status and image. Marlena has nothing left to do but start selling and recruiting others to sell for her. Everything reflects a standard business plan, with incentives and penalties, like most multi-level arrangements offering the average person the chance to make a fortune if they follow all the rules and hit expected sales numbers. The only difference is in the quality of the products themselves. According to anyone who uses them, there's nothing like "Deliciously You" on the market. The sky is the limit if one hustles hard because the products practically sell themselves.

Marlena is overwhelmed but also thrilled at the exciting change in her situation. For the first time in many weeks, she drifts off to a peaceful rest instead of a sleepless night.

She is sipping her first cup of grainy instant coffee because it's all she can currently afford. Marlena boots up her computer, eager to step into her new role as a dedicated influencer. There is a flashing message informing her that her inbox exceeds the limit. Marlena instantly realizes she has several thousand new followers. They all seem eager to know more about the "Deliciously You" products, and many are keen to purchase them as soon as possible. She's stunned and continues clicking through the messages furiously, promising to get back to a few as soon as possible, when her phone trills. Marlena scrambles to answer, but it's at the bottom of her purse. A voicemail recording begins to play when she digs it out, bringing it to life with a tap.

"Hello, this is the office of Dr. Archer Varlow. We're confirming your appointment for tomorrow at 1:30. We look forward to seeing you."

Marlena's head is spinning. She can't remember an appointment, so she presses redial.

"Hello, this is Marlena Bliss. I don't think I have an appointment tomorrow."

"Yes, we have you scheduled; Rafe Bernal's assistant made the appointment for you. We'll see you then." There's a dismissive click. Marlena searches for the physician's name, discovering he's a noted plastic surgeon. What in the hell? She's an average-looking female, but Marlena doesn't often consider altering her appearance besides hating her hips. She taps in her private direct number to the "Deliciously You" home office, and her call connects on the second ring. A female voice with a crisp British accent replies when she asks about the appointment.

"Hello, Marlena. Yes, you have an appointment tomorrow. Rafe insists all of our reps meet his high standards. You'll be having a little touch-up work, but there's no reason to stress. It will only take a couple of hours, and you'll look and feel better. Thanks for calling. Have you received your products yet? My shipping information tells me they are outside your door as we speak. How exciting! Please begin using them immediately, and we'll chat again soon. Have a delicious day!"

She's trying to make sense of it all, it's happening fast, but Marlena is giddy to begin selling products to her dozens of interested potential clients, still blowing up her social media with requests. There are two sizable boxes outside the door of her apartment. Marlena drags them inside, carefully slices through the tape, and scoops out dozens of scented purple tissue paper sheets, finally exposing a generous assortment of lotions and creams. There's also a folder with instruction notes encased in plastic for proper application to achieve the most effective results. She's never been able to afford much in the way of upscale self-care, and Marlena giggles happily as she digs into the first jar, as directed, with the miniature gold spoon provided. As the young woman massages the herb-scented cream onto her face and neck, a strong flush of blood rushes to her cheeks, and her skin tingles as if pinched. Wow. This is potent stuff. I can already feel it working.

Although she has no training in sales and doesn't know how best to market the products presented on her website link, Marlena manages to engage in conversations with dozens of new friends. She secures over a thousand dollars of "Deliciously You" orders on her first day as a rep. It's dark when her stomach growls, reminding her she hasn't had a thing to eat. The sound of bells ding, and Marlena glances at her phone, intending to ignore the tone.

"Incoming Call from Rafe Bernal."

Almost falling out of her chair, Marlena activates the call.

"Hello? I'm Marlena Bliss."

"Yes, hello, beautiful one. I wanted to congratulate you on a brilliant first day with "Deliciously You." Your efforts are appreciated." Hearing his rich and honeyed voice soothes her.

"You're going to be a star, I'm positive. Stay delicious, Marlena. We'll speak again soon."

The young woman relaxes a bit, still processing the effect a brief exchange with Rafe has on her. She's been lonely for a while, it's true. Her last boyfriend was abusive and a cheater, and she's avoided more than a passing connection with anyone else for months. Wrapping her arms around her knees, she shivers, pulling them close. If the man's voice over the phone causes such a profound reaction, Marlena is even more anxious to please her employer in hopes of meeting him.

When Dr. Varlow, the handsome physician, slides a sharp needle deep into the tender flesh of her lips the next day, boosting and plumping them to an exaggerated bee-stung perfection, she shrugs off the pain. Marlena thinks only of how incredible her life will be if she keeps selling at this rate.

Every day brings Marlena new excitement and more sales. Her bank account reflects her growing ability to sell the outstanding product line and herself. The cumulative effects of her new maintenance routine are apparent, her fair complexion shines like never before, and her hair is glossy and thick using the "Deliciously You" line. It's as if she's discovered the fountain of youth at the ripe age of 23, so Marlena is happy to post dozens of selfies daily. She's becoming her own best advertisement. The orders continue to flow in effortlessly, as every young woman wants to look as fabulous as she does in her photos.

Within several weeks, both Marlena's confidence and sales increase substantially. She now owns the latest tech and loves engaging with people worldwide looking to become the best version of themselves by buying her products. She perfects her girl next door client approach and gentle but persuasive selling technique, enabling her to close most sales effortlessly. Company emails sent to her are full of praise and support, and she thrives on the attention. Bonus payments hit her account, and physical perks of designer clothing and accessories show up on her doorstep, but she wears a simple, comfortable dress most of the day as she's glued to her desk. Marlena can now buy a nicer vehicle but has no time to start the process. Each week, she spends her few hours of free time on her upkeep, with regular visits to a nearby hair and nail salon. An exceptional online presence is essential to the "Deliciously You" brand, and she learns to navigate the trappings of the beauty business in a short time.

The company continues to supply her with regular weekly deliveries of products for her use. Marlena notices a slight increase in the percentage of "proprietary active ingredients" listed on the label with each shipment. They are also increasingly expensive, but the sumptuous products' effects on her are now apparent and stunning. She's slimmer, and her body feels firm, although she spends every waking hour sitting at her desk, doing business and selling online. She's seldom hungry and takes a break only when nature calls or the balances and deductions in her account change. Marlena surpasses the higher sales quotas assigned to her, and she understands these numbers are necessary to maintain her status as a top performer.

At a specific prestigious level in the company's pyramid structure, reps must relocate to undisclosed exclusive housing near the company headquarters, labs, and offices. Marlena learns this after the fact. To refuse means an immediate replacement, or a behind-the-scenes position within the company, at a significantly lower salary. Very few eligible reps question this demand, as the financial gains are substantial.

Marlena's ready for a change of scenery and personal life. She spends most of her time in a virtual setting anyway, and her social life is non-existent, so she's excited for a fresh start when DeeDee offers her an attractive relocation package. She packs a few belongings, puts her car in storage, and without a word to anyone, boards a plane to her new address, a tastefully decorated apartment on a tropical beach. Marlena believes this is the start of a life beyond her dreams and continues to work hard. She and Rafe often exchange friendly phone conversations. He's always teasing and light-hearted with Marlena, promising they will eventually meet in person, but currently, his schedule is tight, and he's unavailable.

One morning, the message she's been waiting for arrives.

"Marlena, this is DeeDee. You're doing well. It's time for you to bring others into the fold. Please recruit your first team of lower-tier product reps." Marlena stretches like a cat in her chair, narrowing her eyes at the numbers in her account. She rubs her hands together slowly, admiring her recent manicure. Having others sell under her ensures that her bottom line in terms of profit will continue to build. She can also claim a large percentage of the money brought in by a select few motivated enough to handle the demands of working alone for long hours in front of a computer. Marlena is in a position to earn a lot of money now.

She organizes a virtual meeting with her potential underlings. She'll then be better able to choose among those clamoring for an opportunity to sell the "Deliciously You" line. Marlena issues invitation emails to a diverse group of prospects. They all follow and take an interest in her every move and comment on every post.

Her entire list responds positively and almost immediately; they've been waiting for their time to shine.

Marlena holds court over twenty lovely people at the designated time, each politely desperate to achieve her level of notoriety and financial independence. At a glance, she immediately rules out several based on their appearance alone, then reconsiders one girl who's very animated and bright but not as attractive as the company prefers. There are stringent rules set by "Deliciously You" regarding what one can offer to or demand of her team. Still, there are also provisions in place, should she suggest "physical improvements" befitting the company's image if she feels they can add to her team's bottom line. "Deliciously You" has an account she can access for such things with a simple request.

"Who's ready to change their lives? Are you willing to do what's necessary? Are you ready to have it all? You can be the envy of everyone who sees you, and in return for working and selling products with me, you will gain a huge following and so many fans! We know it's all about those "likes and buys," so who's with me?"

Marlena feeds off the group's energy and nervous responses to her questions. She's never been so popular, and it's an adrenaline rush! Everyone wants to be on her team, and a few are reduced to tears as they emotionally describe what the chance to work with her means to them. She wants to sign them all up, thinking of all the delicious money she can make but decides instead to add four on the spot, to appear more exclusive. Each person she chooses has hundreds of followers and friends on their social media pages, translating to high initial sales for her. They are also active on their media platforms at all hours of the day and night. The company now includes a refreshing complimentary tea flavored with natural mint and herbs in her deliveries, intended to help her stay alert and awake longer. Marlena drinks several cups a day, and it makes a difference. She doesn't require much sleep anymore.

"Thank you all for your interest. I've chosen those I feel are a great fit based on this panel discussion. If you're not selected this time, I'll be looking for my second-tier folks soon, so visit my pages often for updates. Oh, and be sure to stock up on your "Deliciously You" products. This week's special is our dreamy "You Dew You" body cream. I promise you'll be wearing the best skin of your life." Marlena winks playfully at the anxious faces in gallery mode on her screen, then blows a kiss as the connection fades to black for all but four of the faces.

Darla. Evan. Rita. Juliette. Her new team members are squealing with excitement. They're loudly chattering and congratulating each other when Marlena raises a finger to silence them. Rafe's direct number repeatedly flashes on her phone as if the device itself is annoyed with her. She needs to return his call.

"It's lovely to have you onboard, and I'll reach out to you personally later this evening. Be expecting your first weekly shipment of our glorious products within a couple of days. You all must start using them immediately. Your personal sales portals will be live within the hour so you can review information, transfer funds, and get yourselves set up and ready to begin making sales as soon as tomorrow, with approval." Marlena's hand flutters goodbye like a prom queen on a parade float, waving to fans. Dismissing the group with a single click of her keyboard, she wonders if four recruits are enough. Did she underestimate her own sales potential? She notices her fingers, decorated with three slim gold rings she gifted herself after an impressive month, shake slightly. I need less tea and more sleep. Marlena grits her teeth, then sighs. There's a business call requiring her attention. She'll try to rest later.

The tired young woman replaces her noise-blocking headset. When she's not actively selling products, she listens to motivational recordings and examples of sales pitches for "Deliciously You" products. She's been ignoring her few friends for weeks, and most have stopped calling since she moved away. There's a television mounted on one wall, but Marlena can't recall the last time she watched anything or listened to current events.

"Sacrifice Is Greatness." The recording sent to her last week stuck in her mind, and Marlena intends to listen to this session again, reminding herself why she needs to focus. It's all about goals, hers and those of the company. Both are set almost impossibly high. The ring tone is shrill when she dials her boss back. The line engages, but there's no warm greeting when he answers. There's no response.

Marlena can hear Rafe's controlled breathing on the other end of the line. It's unsettling.

"Rafe? It's Marlena returning your call." Marlena is unusually nervous about speaking with her boss and doesn't know why. "I have four brilliant and beautiful new team members, and I'm anticipating my best month ever." She smiles, hoping her words are enough to please her increasingly demanding employer. Rubbing the back of her neck, Marlena shifts in her chair as an uncomfortable silence continues.

"You disappoint me, Marlena." Rafe's typically smooth voice is a low snarl. "You can do better and more. DeeDee told you to select a team, not have a tea party. I'm withholding next week's product shipment and reducing your sales and profits by ten percent until you prove you're willing to work harder." The phone clicks in Marlena's ear before she can reply. Her mouth is dry, and her lower lip cracks slightly when her teeth bite into it hard to keep from crying.

I have to make this better. I'll find a way to make Rafe happy again.

Flinching and sniffing, Marlena sets up her equipment, touches up her makeup, and puts on her game face. Professional lighting reflects a perfect image of her on the screen. She hits a "Go Live" button on her page, which is already full of curious new shoppers watching videos and adoring devotees wanting to be the first to try any new products. They are pleasantly surprised and virtually greet Marlena, applauding her random arrival.

"Hello, everyone. I'm delighted you're here, and for the next few minutes, I'm discounting all of our popular "Angel Glow" serums for an unheard-of twenty percent off." Chimes echo in the room as dozens of sales register immediately. "Also, I'm looking for ten more special friends and fans to join my sales team. Email me right away if you think you'd be a good fit." She's careful not to stay on for too long. She can't risk anyone tracking or hacking her account. "Deliciously You" demands privacy and discretion in all of its business dealings, including where the headquarters and representatives are located, for security reasons. Dozens respond to her call for more people to join her team, and Marlena stays up the rest of the night, selecting, then having conversations with her new members. The days ahead will force her to push herself and her hand-picked team to new heights in sales. Marlena is determined to redeem herself with her boss. She's hungry for his approval and all he can continue to offer.

But instead of feeling newly motivated and excited, the successful but emotionally isolated young woman regrets her choices. Her so-called team proves to be anything but one.

Marlena's confidence takes a hit, and she now doubts her ability to maintain her sales and meet quotas. Her more significant but non-cohesive team selling under her doesn't listen to her prerecorded mentoring sessions, and they don't bother logging into her mandatory meetings. They all ignore her for the most part. They are ungrateful, greedy, and chewing at her heels while trying to bring her down so they can rise. They are more interested in a fat bank balance than building client loyalty and gaining repeat customers who order regularly.

One, in particular, Juliette, misrepresents the acceptable "Deliciously You" product claims, resulting in a handful of negative reviews front and center on the company home page. Several bully clients into purchasing large amounts of products with expiration dates. Some precious active ingredients "go bad" and develop a rancid odor before they can use them. For the first time in the company's venerable history, projected sales quotas fall short.

And it's all Marlena's fault.

Marlena can't control or communicate effectively with her recruits; they have their agendas, seeking recognition and fortunes as rivals, not as team players under her umbrella. It's not the way it's supposed to work. She didn't expect this to happen.

Marlena is resentful her piece of the pie chart grows smaller instead of larger.

There have been no calls from the home office or encouraging messages from Rafe Bernal. His private number is no longer in service, and Marlena can't access the personal page on the company website with contact information. She's locked out completely. She's been left out in the cold to figure things out independently, without support, until her sales increase and she can produce at an impressive level again. The weekly shipment of products she's come to rely on is on hold. She can feel and see the difference in her physical appearance, her complexion is matte and dull, and strands of hair clog her brush, it's thinning dramatically. She has tiny cracks on her forehead and around her lips, adding years to her face. They grow more noticeable by the day. Marlena isn't shining as bright, and she needs to do something to bring her sales back on track. Her looks and her bank balance are declining at a rapid pace. She's also being docked a high percentage for each sales period she doesn't meet her quota.

There's a ping. Evan, a team member, needs a few days off to attend a family event, and he wants Marlena to approve a leave of absence. She has no experience with the process. Sales have been her entire focus, not managing people. Marlena connects with DeeDee, who is still her assigned go-to for details and protocol.

"Marlena. What can I do for you?" DeeDee's voice sounds computer-generated and automatic today. "I'm busy, so please get to the point." What a difference from the chirpy and gossipy conversations they've had. Marlena bites the inside of her cheek, then forces a laugh.

"So nice to connect. I have a team member who needs to take some time off. A few days. Is this acceptable?" Marlena has never taken a day off, so she's unfamiliar with the process.

"Please hold." Uplifting instrumental music blasts into Marlena's ear. She clears her throat several times, anticipating DeeDee's response.

"Hello, Marlena." Rafe sounds like his old self again; his voice is syrupy and calm. "I'd like you to come over to the main office, shall we say, in an hour or so? I'll see you then." Goosebumps cover Marlena's arms. She's lived near the expansive "Deliciously You" headquarters for quite a while and has never set foot inside the gate.

There's not much time, so Marlena ties back her hair, then scrapes around the edges of her last jar of "Baby, You're Beautiful," rubbing the gritty product against her face. It's a miracle cleanser, instantly rinsing away signs of stress and fatigue. She adds a bit of makeup, then slides into an effortlessly chic black designer dress. Marlena's weight has shifted. It's much tighter than she remembers. She's tugging at the hem, uncomfortable in her ensemble, as she leaves her apartment for the first time in weeks. The fresh air and daylight feel good, but there's no time to enjoy them. Wiggling into the front seat of her car, she's hopeful Rafe will not only sympathize with her current fall from grace but will also give her a chance to prove she's still worthy.

Two large cast-iron gates, heavily embossed with flowers and angel wings, automatically swing open as Marlena slows to a crawl at the entrance. Low-profile buildings with glaring sunproof glass line both sides of a narrow driveway that leads to the main offices. According to the Property Map, this information flickers on her GPS screen. Marlena chews at a hangnail. Her nerves are on edge as she parks, then walks to the door. There's a brass buzzer embedded in the rock wall. The door opens instantly when she barely touches it, and a beautiful young woman with blue eyes wearing a pressed white lab coat greets her.

"I'm DeeDee. Please come in. He's waiting." Marlena's palms are damp, so she doesn't extend a hand.

"I'm so happy to..." DeeDee ignores the girl, and her look of contempt rushes over Marlena like a wave. She follows the voice she knows only from phone calls into an office. Rafe Bernal stands with his back to them, looking out a window.

"DeeDee tells me there are problems, Marlena. Your team is a problem, and that makes you a problem. Your sales are falling, and you're failing my trust in you." Rafe turns to face Marlena. He's handsome in a frozen-mask sort of way, but there's no vitality to his features, and he's not nearly as attractive as his persona online. His hair is his best feature, thick and black, covering his shoulders. No one would expect he's the mastermind behind a billion-dollar marketing empire. The slim man is wearing black pants and a sweatshirt with a hood covering his neck to his ears. He's not someone you'd glance twice at in passing.

His dark eyes are flat, and the heavy brows above knit close together in a frown. Marlena gulps back her apprehension, glancing around the room, trying not to break down crying. A chilling line of perspiration dribbles down between her breasts. She's feverish and clammy all over.

"I want you to keep your position with the company, Marlena, but this meeting will serve as your only and final warning. You've been invested in and received products and perks, and until recently, you've made us some money. I will advise you of your options, and you can choose your future for yourself." Rafe walks out into the hallway, beckoning Marlena to follow. She trips on the edge of a rug, steadies herself, and waits while he unlocks the door leading into a large room. It takes all of her composure to follow the grim male inside.

"This is one of our production rooms. Take a good look around." Long metal tables line the walls on all sides. Precisely calibrated equipment sliding overhead squeezes pale pink cream into glass jars. Marlena inhales. Her eyes are wide. The workers, wearing white lab coats, are seated at the tables. They carefully smooth the top of the cream, then add gilt lids. All are desiccated, shriveled, and bent over skin shells, resembling humans. They make no sound, going through the motions of their task without emotion or an indication they are alive. She's digging her fingernails into her palms, hands clenched at her sides. They all look exactly alike.

Are they diseased? Are they contagious? Marlena's struggling to breathe. She can barely make out Rafe's words.

"You can step down, Marlena. DeeDee believes Rita will make an excellent team leader. Why she's already recruiting members of her family, and her sales are exemplary. "Deliciously You" doesn't offer severance or have retirement provisions. You choose to give up your life, friends, family, time, and everything that makes you who you are, pursuing adoration, instant fame, and money. So, when you are no longer willing or able to meet my expectations, I will take you and use what's left until there is nothing. I have an endless supply of free labor because of so many people like you!"

Rafe gestures casually around the room. The workers are unresponsive. "Even your dust is used to polish the machines." Rafe's laughter fills the silent room, but there's no joy in the sound. "You pathetic creatures, lusting after attention and craving the likes and approval. You exist only as long as the adoration of others validates you. Your greed and need are so great that I've been able to exist for hundreds of years. "Deliciously You" is only my latest success story. He's clutching Marlena's arm, roughly supporting her. The girl's body is bent over, her head in her hands. Tears splashed onto the concrete floor.

"Tears, my dear? Did you cry when Mrs. Cullen couldn't afford her products anymore? Or when Darla, have you noticed she's gone missing, gave up entirely, bowing to the pressure you piled on her, more and more every week? You've seen what happens when clients stop using their precious "Deliciously You" goodies. I've designed the products to bring out the best and the worst in people; you've had only a tiny taste of the cellular damage they eventually cause but take another look around." Marlena is sobbing now, unable to control her fear. Her unquenchable thirst for wealth and success has brought unspeakable horror to herself and others.

"Did you ever think to ask about those "proprietary ingredients?" The active ones increasing in potency with each client's delivery. Some refer to them as "stem cells," but I like to think of them as offerings. We can remove these additional ingredients, painfully, I regret to say. The final results aren't pretty." Rafe laughs again, pointing at one of the hideous workers. "Everyone feeds on something or someone because they dread any kind of rejection or cancellation. I feed on the energy of fresh blood, so eager and willing to please, regardless of the price. Everyone sells out eventually. Stop sniveling Marlena. You have two choices. Meet your damn quotas, keep selling "Deliciously You" like I know you can, and continue living an enviable life or retire immediately. There's a spot at my table waiting for you." Rafe's face twists into a vicious smirk. He's amused at his joke. Leaning in, he kisses Marlena's cheek. "DeeDee with see you out. Have a delicious day, my dear." With a flip of his hair, he's gone. The hallway reeks of sulfur. Marlena staggers out behind DeeDee, who refuses to make eye contact with the broken young woman.

"I will assume you're good to go. Be sure to check your portal when you get home; there will be changes in your percentage and quotas." DeeDee strolls away. Marlena yanks open the door to her car, wanting to get as far away from the "Deliciously You" headquarters as fast as possible.

Marlena returns to her desk, still in shock, but she's anxious to redeem herself. There's no other option. Her inbox is blinking, full of new messages and orders. She can once again access her portal. Her quota for this week is lower than usual. Rafe is granting her a second chance. She digs the toes of her bare feet firmly into the plush carpet, determined to do well. Marlena pushes up her sleeves and clicks on her filtering light. Her image is polished and beautiful when she answers the first message. The camera loves her, and

Marlena relaxes into her familiar pitch when a well-groomed woman with silver hair answers her call.

"Hello, Mrs. Reed. It's so nice to connect. I have a special deal for you. My favorite product, our "Deliciously You Ever Young" body cream, is two jars for today's price only. Let me describe the effects, they are remarkable, and I know you'll want to have a supply on hand. I can't live without it." Marlena smiles. Mrs. Reed's eyes glow with excitement at the promise of having more supple skin. She hungers to be young again, no matter the cost.

WRECKERS

KENZIE JENNINGS

IT HAD ALWAYS BEEN about love for Jasper Dratch.

He was just that kind of romantic. The problem though was that Jasper was more inclined to devote his heart to objects rather than people. Beautiful, expensive objects.

Taylor, "Tay," Holden used to be that shiny object.

She'd been carefully sculpted and waxed, tanned and plumped in all the right places, just the way Jasper liked it.

Well, Jasper AND Taylor's 1.8 million Instagram followers.

Today though, Jasper had eyes for only one, and that wasn't Taylor. It was fine, really. She understood.

"Haaaaaay! Y'all wanted to see it. THIS is what Jasper bought today," Taylor said, beaming into her cell lens. She panned past Jasper who was talking with the car dealer. She pointed with a gem-encrusted claw, and her camera automatically zoomed in on his new lady, a Ferrari F8 Tributo in Giallo Modena ("Yellow like a bee?" Taylor had pressed. "Yellow like Italian, Tay," Jasper had corrected.).

As soon as they had arrived at the dealership to pick up Jasper's love, Jasper couldn't have been more excited to preen over her and ride her until she had the life sucked right out of her.

To be perfectly frank, Taylor wouldn't have been a bit surprised if he really had been fucking any of his cars since their sex life had dwindled lately to nothing more than jacking off over Taylor's recently updated 34DDs. It was a routine that had grated Taylor's nerves like anything else Jasper did with her and anything else he did to her.

It wouldn't last.

"I mean, I kinda get it," Taylor continued to her followers, holding her cell up so that it was perfectly angled to capture both her sparkling smile and deep cleavage. "I dropped a couple thou last week at Sephora. Like you go in for one thing and come out with, like, twenty moisturizers and palettes and lipsticks..."

She could hear Jasper and the salesman titter from across the showroom floor. "Tay, this isn't lipstick. It's a three hundred thousand dollar diamond on the road," said Jasper. He turned back to the salesman, their voices low, their words jumbled white noise. It was often the case with guys and their toys.

Taylor hustled towards her boyfriend, her high heels clicking a rapid staccato on the shiny linoleum. "I'm just saying I get why you like what you like, and no matter what, it's going to be good quality. I mean, we get what we pay for," she said, waving her hand in the car's direction. "Amazing quality, right? We're privileged that way."

However, Jasper's full attention was on the key fob the salesman was dangling in front of Jasper's line of sight.

Taylor rolled her eyes at her cell, that sort of look that would inevitably garner responses from hundreds of empathetic followers whose partners were often distracted by shiny things.

Those things.

Too many things.

And none of it was ever enough for a guy like Jasper Dratch.

As if on cue, Jasper was at his girlfriend's side, making sure Taylor's audience would see the sloppy smooch he planted on her cheek. He playfully spun her, grabbing her around her tiny waist, her heavy designer tote smacking her thigh with the sudden movement. He then pulled her in for a real kiss, even while she kept the cell at an arm's length, still recording for everyone to see their passion for each other.

Even if it was just as manufactured as anything else around them.

Taylor knew. She always had.

JASPER WAS HAVING way too much fun behind the wheel of his new plaything. His intent was to test his angel's limits on the coastal highway, like all the rich idiot daredevils before him. Normally, Taylor would've been wound tightly, her back pressed against the seat, one hand gripping the handle above the passenger door.

Normally, certainly.

However, from the passenger side, Taylor calmly reapplied her lipstick, even leaning to one side as the car sharply swerved. She was practiced at her primping. Once, she'd been on a redeye from coast to coast, and the flight got caught in an air pocket that for anyone else touching up their face, would've been a cosmetic disaster, lipstick streaked everywhere.

"I'm telling you, girl," Jasper said, "there's nothing like this. That feeling you get when you drive, and the world's nothing but a blur outside your bubble. You hear that?"

"Hear what?"

He grinned. "Exactly," He stole a glance at Taylor. "So smooth. Finest whiskey on wheels."

"But she's Italian, Jas."

Jasper made a face. "So?"

"It's a terrible analogy."

"Who the fuck asked you?"

"I'm just saying." Taylor flipped up the visor and dropped her lipstick in her bag. With her cell in one hand, she opened the tote wide with the other and rummaged around in its depths.

Jasper gritted his teeth as he gave the car more gas, forcing it to move faster on the highway's curves. "You know something, Tay? We need to talk about the next steps," he said.

"Next steps to what?" Taylor muttered. She was only paying him partial attention. She seemed more interested in finding whatever it was she was looking for in her bag.

"You and me. Where are we going with this? We've been together for what, a couple months, right? I think we should take a break."

Taylor's eyes flickered for a second, but only a second. Whatever it was she had been looking for, she found it and smiled to herself. She then hit the record button on her cell camera.

She pouted prettily into the lens. "Hey, you guys. Such a sad day here in Taylor land..."

"More like lalaland," Jasper muttered.

Taylor rolled down the passenger window and then shot him a glare before clearing her throat and continuing. "So this just happened: Jasper broke up with me seconds ago...right here...in his brand new Ferrari...while we're driving on one of the most dangerous roads on the coast."

"I just said we needed a break, Tay."

"But what Jasper doesn't get is that he thinks this is gonna affect me somehow, like my life will shatter or something if I don't have him and his dad's money around anymore." Taylor's sad pout twisted into a wide leer, the skin of her face shifting as if pulled by invisible hooks. Her tone also shifted, growing thick and dark. "I don't care about money or status or any of this Instabullshit. I especially don't give a fuck about any of you. You're nothing but a blight on society. Scrolling for a quick fix, whatever the latest trend is, whoever is on display at your beck and call."

Jasper had gone quiet at her words. He'd felt the air around them shift, or was it the hairs prickling on his skin, warning him that something wasn't right?

This wasn't the Taylor he knew.

"Tay..." He glanced down at her lap. In between everything, she'd somehow managed to pull out a revolver from her bag without him noticing. The bag itself had been placed at her feet, the gun curled in her hand in her lap. "What are you—?"

Whatever he'd wanted to say had caught in his throat as Taylor casually aimed the gun at his temple. He felt the chill of the muzzle pressing deeply against his skin, tunneling an indentation there.

"That's the problem with the world today," Taylor said. "It's all about consuming as much space and resources as we can, and we just keep destroying anything in our way." Even though she had the gun right at Jasper's temple, she kept filming, focusing on Jasper's face that had gone grey.

"What's with the gun, Tay? You don't need that. What do you want me to do? I can do whatever you want, baby," Jasper's words came out in a stream of panic. His voice had turned gratingly shrill.

"In less than a century, we will have raped the land entirely," she continued. "I don't know about you, but I don't want to live in a world where greed is what kills us in the end. I want us to be able to go out on our own terms, leaving the earth to heal without anymore human interference—"

"Tay, you're acting crazy. Put down the gun. I've slowed down. See? And I can pull off to the side of the road here, and we can talk about your issues. Anything you want…"

"—As a member of The Square, I do this of my own free will," Taylor said just before she fired, the shot splattering blood and bits of skull and brain matter all over the driver window and door.

Right before Jasper's precious new Ferrari crashed against the barricade ahead of them and soared, pummeling over the edge of the rocky cliffside, Taylor had tossed her cell out the window so that it clattered onto the asphalt of the road.

Aside from that one trace of their existence before they died in a fiery crash, there was little left that was recognizable of Jasper Dratch and Taylor Holden.

At that point, Taylor had reached up to 37k reactions.

By the early hours of the morning, she'd gained 380k new followers.

And it seemed as if the entire world had begun its collective web search of The Square.

For those who knew, Taylor had done her due diligence.

SHE'D BEEN A GIRL, no more than sixteen...seventeen. The third one I'd seen in person since this all started happening.

She'd not worn a helmet. Her once unicorn-colored, spiky haircut was matted with blood. She might have been conventionally pretty, but it was hard to tell. Her face was a raw mask of scraped meat and exposed teeth, having been sloughed away against the concrete. Within seconds, she'd become a graphic poster child for motorcycle safety. A case of lethal road rash and broken bones.

But this girl, she wouldn't ever be a statistic.

The car that had struck her, running headlong into her on that country road, had been nothing more than an ordinary SUV that had promptly driven right into a utility pole afterwards. The woman who'd been behind the wheel hadn't been wearing a seat-belt. The M.E. on site and a couple of other plainclothes were examining her body.

"It was deliberate again. Driver knew what she was doing," Cortez said, nudging me with her boot. "Kit, you okay? Look a little shell-shocked."

I couldn't form words. I couldn't think of them. I kept looking from each angle, then back to the girl, then back around, my thoughts spinning. Any of my colleagues at the Center would've stated the obvious. The post-traumatic stress, always at the root, caused my words to turn to mush in my head.

I still couldn't shake the sight of car wreck victims even though I'd been one myself.

A stray plank that had loosened from a pickup truck bed had decimated my mother's head. None of the planks had been properly secured, so when the driver nearly missed the line of traffic at the red light and suddenly slammed on his brake, the plank shot out and hit my mother's windshield, crashing through it and then my mother's face, like something out of a horror movie.

I'd been seven years old, sitting behind the front passenger seat. It's one of the earliest memories I have of my mother, and it's why I am the way I am. Therapists and school counselors and teachers and professors and well-meaning friends and neighbors have all tried to keep my rattled nerves settled, but there's nothing that can shake that deep rooted anxiety that has long burrowed knots into your soul.

The truth was, I may never get over the carnage The Square was ultimately responsible for. This kind of murder-suicide was horrific. For me, it let that anxiety deep down sprout thorns all over.

One of the other officers strolled over and handed Cortez something. "Like the others," he said before he turned back to questioning the witnesses on the scene.

Cortez held up what he'd handed her, a red cell phone.

Like the others.

"Shall I do the honors?" she said.

"By all means." It wasn't like we didn't know what we'd see.

The uploaded videos were often the last course of action the members of The Square took before crashing their cars, killing themselves and other people in the process. And they all filmed their manifestos on brick red smartphones.

This time, the driver had actually been a soccer mom type with layered blonde hair freshly highlighted and a face with apple cheeks and smile lines crinkling around her blue eyes. She was driving, her focus on the road ahead. Her phone had filmed her from the dashboard. She'd likely had it there originally to film near-accidents she would've reported. Normally, members of The Square made a production of it, their cells set up to get the perfect angle with the perfect amount of natural light, quite often when their cars were parked somewhere before the members drove into oncoming traffic or off bridges.

"I have five kids," she said, her concentrated scowl furrowing. "I can't live like this. I can't live in a place where I know they're gonna have to deal with rising waters, flash floods, wildfires burning down whole communities... I'm already feeling like I'm the one responsible. Like I'm the one who added to the problems just by having so many kids. And I am so sorry." The woman had already started to tear up, her voice wavering, breaking her steadfast shell. "Mike, if you ever see this, and I know you will...the police are gonna show it to you... We should never have agreed to have a family." She sighed. "But we did, and there's nothing we can do about it now. Our children are going to pay for the consequences of our decisions."

"Your children are going to be motherless," Cortez muttered to the woman on the cell's screen, as if she was listening. "How you feel about that? How can she not feel any guilt about what she's doing?"

The Center had sent some of my colleagues into the field across the U.S. for this very reason. The cases assigned to me just happened to be in my county, hardly much of a drive away from my home.

We were treated as if we had the logical answers for any of this happening, as if we could answer such questions easily. It was all about brainwashing, repeated ideas and beliefs, incoming messages relaying the same thing over and over and over again until the listener began to understand what the messenger was really trying to communicate.

For The Square, the message was clear:

Death by the one creation that symbolized American exceptionalism, the one creation that had us reliant and co-dependent, and the one creation that would cause enough horror to warn us of our own impending self-destruction if we kept expanding the population.

Simply put, death by automobile.

The driver continued, ending her tirade in the same way as all the others: "As a member of The Square, I do this of my own free will."

She then reached over and shut off her cell.

Cortez circled around, looking over at the scene once again, before she faced me. "She's the fifth in two weeks now," she said. "This town is barely a dot on a map. Everyone is everyone else's neighbor. They know each other's business. What if they're all part of this this, too?"

"An entire town of followers?" As soon as I said it, I realized it was conceivable, and it made a heck of a lot of sense for the Center to keep me here.

A couple of fire fighters were working to get the driver's body free from the broken windshield. She was caught halfway in the loose web of shattered glass. There were clusters of rubberneckers gaping at the sight and talking amongst themselves. One group in particular caught my attention. A trio of middle-aged women, suburban types, had broken away from the scene to huddle together in a tight formation.

I excused myself to Cortez and made my way over to them. They had been in the middle of a heated discussion when one of them—a tall, hard-faced redhead who seemed to command the others' attention—saw me approaching and hushed the other two, nodding in my direction.

She didn't know that I'd caught something she'd said just before the group turned silent. Brief, but clear enough that I'd store it away to look up. A name.

"Hi there." I figured I'd try my hand at being warm and approachable, even while my stomach was in knots. "Did any of you ladies know her?"

"She's not a cop," one of them muttered.

The redhead smirked in my direction. "Then we don't have to talk to her, do we?"

"Who's that you mentioned, Geraldine Haines?"

That got their attention, the fact that I'd heard them. The three of them looked as if they just realized they'd all eaten a cockroach.

"Don't blame me for asking," I said, keeping the calm in my voice nice and steady. I kept my focus solely on the redhead. "You brought her up. She have something to do with this?"

Their silence trickled stinging icy water through my veins.

"I take it she's local? Did she know the driver here?"

"Go fuck yourself," the redhead said around a sneer. She signaled with a head nod to her friends, and they turned and made their way back to the cars that had been parked on the grass past the taped off barricade around the scene.

I'd find out on my own, of course. It's what I do. However, a timer had already been set in motion, and I wasn't ready to find out the rest.

I wasn't ready at all.

By the time I was back at the house, my laptop growing hot on the desk, I'd familiarized myself with a one Geraldine Haines. Since she was local, she wasn't hard to find, but when I first saw her profile and went through her social media presence, it didn't appear to me as if she was anything more than a happy-looking, 60-something year old librarian with her colorful tops, dangly earrings, and cheerful smile. Frankly, she was impressive. She'd won several awards for her research in children's literacy. Plus, she was obviously active and beloved in the community. There were dozen of photos of her in various costumes reading to kids circled around her feet. Other pictures had her in evening wear, holding a barely touched glass of wine and smiling while standing next to the business elite at local charity functions.

Even her Facebook feed, on first glance, seemed devoid of any red flags. Not like anything had been regularly updated. She tended to post photos more than anything else. However, there were lots of old birthday messages and tagged posts about libraries and literature. After a bit of scrolling, I managed to finally find something useful. At least, I thought it was.

The post on her page was from an anonymous source with an

American flag with an empty square where the stars should've been as the profile picture.

It simply read The Great Renewal has begun and was dated two months prior to my search, on January 25th of this year.

Anyone who'd been paying close attention to what had been happening across the country would know perfectly well that January 25th was the date when Taylor Holden, the Instagram star, had recited a carefully phrased manifesto from inside her boyfriend's new Ferrari, the chilling finality of it having become familiar all across the U.S. and the rest of the world by now. Then she promptly blew her boyfriend's brains out and steered the car off a cliff.

That event was just the start. Those of us at the Center had been paying close attention once the numbers of traffic fatalities began to climb…and climb…

We knew.

We just knew it was indoctrination.

And the more info. I dug up about Ms. Haines, the more I wished I didn't know a damned thing.

IT WASN'T the alarm that jerked me awake. It was something primal, something dark and maternal that I'd not experienced since Micah —Marbles to the rest of us—had almost suffocated in his sleep when he was a baby. The only light in the bedroom turned the area by my side of the bed a dusky red, the glow from the digital clock that read it was 5:42am. Even the sleep meds hadn't given me sanctuary on such nights when I knew, I could feel something wrong, something lurking there in my bones.

Waylon calls it my "itchy instinct." He, on the other hand, was sunken in sleep, his snores rumbling and wet. I sat up in bed, taking care not to move too quickly because if he got up, he'd be in a terrible mood for the rest of the day. That man and his sleep.

Not a peep from down the hallway either. Like father like son, that sleep. Marbles started snoring when he was five, which has weirdly soothed me. It's like whenever I hear it coming from him, I know he's breathing at least.

The only sounds were the sporadic clicking of the ice-maker and the wind rustling the leaves outside the bedroom window.

My cell suddenly buzzed on the nightstand, rattling its impatience and gall. I grabbed it and answered before it could break Waylon out of his slumber. I hadn't needed to see who it was.

It was my Itchy Instinct calling, and it lodged a stone in my throat. My voice came out raspy. "This is Kit."

"Hey, I know it's early," Cortez said on the other end. She sounded as if she'd been alert all night. "...but she's here, and we may not be able to hold her, depending on what happens with her. I'm doing my best, but with all the bureaucratic red tape involved, it gets harder to work with what I'm allotted."

When I feel fear, it's dipped in ice water and then trickling down my back. "I'll be there as soon as I can. Twenty minutes tops."

"Kit, she came willingly, like she's been ready to talk."

That ice water, it stung my throat, and my heartbeat felt as if it had stopped. I exhaled slowly into the phone and then swallowed before I asked, "Has she called anyone yet?"

"She hasn't asked to."

"Whatever you do, don't let anyone talk to her if you can help it. Do not, under any circumstances, speak to her yourself. Understand?"

Cortez went quiet on the other end. I could hear her breathing, the shaking whisper of it there, subtle, but I caught it.

"I need you to say you understand."

"I understand. I wasn't going to," she said softly. "The thought of being alone in a room with someone like her scares the shit out of me, and hell, I've interrogated murder suspects and rapists... pedophiles...you name it. "

"She's not the same."

"No..." Cortez took a deep breath. "No, she is not."

"If anyone brings her coffee or anything else, they go in in pairs. No one goes in alone with her. No one but me. I mean it."

After I'd hung up and quickly dressed, I gave the snoring menace a quick peck on the top of his head, which caused him to stir from his sleep and groggily wake. I was pulling on my boots by the time Waylon had switched on the nightstand lamp and was sitting up, blinking away the sleep from his eyes. His favorite tee shirt that had fast become his favorite sleep shirt had a cartoon Han and Lando grinning at each other, high-fiving, their faces folded from deep creases in the shirt fabric.

"Can you take little man to school on your way in?" I said, grabbing my purse from the armchair.

"Yeah, I figured you'd ask," Waylon said around a yawn. "Why the hell they calling you in so early?"

"Cortez says she's at the station."

That woke him up. He shifted in the bed, going stiff-backed against the headboard. "Serious? What, she just turned herself in?"

"I don't know."

"She suddenly get a conscience at six in the morning?"

Waylon was into details. The way he parsed the truth was to poke at it until something eventually relented. We fell in love over trivia night at the Ale House downtown. He just wouldn't stop questioning each answer that was correct, and when I told him sometimes, the end of the matter was just that (well, that, and he needed to shut up), he turned to stare at me with those tiger eyes of his, and that was it for us.

I blew him a kiss, which he caught in his hand and smacked on his cheek. He knew full well that I don't play Answer The Barrage of Questions, especially that early in the morning.

"Don't take the long way on the interstate. He'll be late if you do!" I shouted on my way out the front door.

"Got it, m' lady!"

THE ITCHY INSTINCT had gone bone chillingly cold by the time I reached the interstate overpass. I used to enjoy early morning drives because I liked the quiet solitude of it and that sense of comfort in knowing everyone else was tucked away at home, still sleeping or getting ready for the day.

Ever since I learned of the existence of Geraldine Haines, however, I prefer the sanctuary of home, our Marbles safe and sound with me and Waylon, hidden away from the real monsters like her lurking there in the dark.

My cell buzzed awake in my bag. It was Cortez again. That prickle over my skin felt like icy needles poking through. I didn't want to answer. I didn't want to hear. I wanted to turn the car around and head back to my husband, my kid, my world. She was persistent though, demanding I answer. When I finally did, she sounded breathless on the other end.

"There's something you should know before you get here."

The warning in her tone. That Itchy Instinct poking at me to make the U-turn.

"Kit, she asked for you specifically."

I supposed I shouldn't have been surprised even though I was, and the thought of it terrified me. I'm only hired to do what I do, and around here, I'm the only one who is willing to attempt it. My track record was spotty at best, but it's the nature of the work.

"Anyone can Google any of us from the Center, and we all know how savvy she is. I mean, she's a librarian who's done a lot of scholarly research. She'd be an idiot if she hadn't looked me up, and it helps that I'm local," I said. I was almost at the turn to the station, and by then, my speed was at a turtle-crawl.

"I know, but this is different. She wanted to know if you'd be bringing in those seven layer cookies that you make when you're trying to calm everyone down."

My breath caught in my throat. I pulled the car over and put it in Park, letting the motor grumble. I internally scrolled through a list of all of the possible reasons why and how she'd know about such a small, intricate detail, something so frivolous as baking something sweet to make everyone happy when things were tense.

Something specific.

There were several logical possibilities, none of which eased my jangled nerves. In fact, they were each horrifying to contemplate:

A)There was a mole, a member of the Square, who had infiltrated the local police station where I'd brought in those cookies on a particularly awful day when the fourth car crash occurred.

B)They'd been in my house and had bugged it.

C)(The worst to contemplate) They were still IN my house.

"Kit? You still there?"

"Give me a second." I couldn't stop trembling.

Bless the woman for being two steps ahead. She said, "I've sent a car to your house. They're on night shift anyway, so they could use the excitement."

I finally exhaled. It came out ragged. "Thank you. Waylon should be up. Once he's awake, he doesn't go back to sleep."

"No problem."

"What's she doing now? Are you where you can see her?"

"She's just sitting there, sipping her coffee. She's asked for the crossword book she keeps in her purse, but there's no way I am letting her have anything to write with."

"Let her have it."

"What? Why? She could use it as a weapon. We don't let people like this have any access to—"

"Just let her," I said. "Believe me. The more she's mentally occupied, the easier it is to keep her quiet. If she has any interaction, any attempt to talk to anyone there, that's when I'd worry."

I wasn't in any mood to argue, but Ms. Haines didn't seem the kind of dangerous woman who'd wield weapons. Others like, quite possibly, one of her own at the station, they could be signaled.

That's why it was vital to keep her distracted, even if for the time I'd finally got in.

The Square's spread had reached across the entirety of the U.S. like a virus. That sort of brainwashing dug deep, worming its way through the mind, leaving its slime to fester in all of the cracks where one's awful memories of childhood trauma paired with all the adult secrets had been dormant. All it needed to pollinate was a leader who was relentless in her quest for some form of annihilation. For someone like Ms. Haines and her cohorts, that would most certainly be a car crash.

I pulled back on the road, drove a little further, and then turned into the parking lot. When I left my car and headed into the station, it felt as if I was walking into the nothing that was the echoing hallow of death. The place was shrouded in silence. The only sign of life there was a gaunt-faced man sleeping soundly on a line of chairs, like a makeshift bed. He'd cocooned himself in a puffy coat, one arm acting as a pillow, the other hand tucked under his chin.

I made my way to the reception area. Its desk was unmanned, which, I suppose, made sense since it was still the night shift. Normally, the lone cop on duty would be in charge, which meant that he or she would've had to take care of anyone coming in.

However, it didn't help ease the terror that had consumed me since Cortez's call at nearly six in the morning. If anything, it made it worse.

I sent both Waylon and Cortez a quick text, letting them know I was there. It didn't take long before the double doors to the hallway in the back buzzed, signaling they were unlocked, and then they clicked. My hand on the push handle, I took a deep breath before heading through.

I swear, I heard the sound of a man's laugh, a low rumble, coming from the reception area behind me. I spun around as the doors swung shut. Through the doors' windows, I snatched a glance at the man in the puffy jacket standing there right in front of the doors, staring at me, a grin stretching his pockmarked cheeks. He gave me a jaunty wave, wiggling his fingers as he did. Didn't take much for me to turn back around and high tail it down the hall.

"You know you've got a guy out front...?" I said upon meeting Cortez at the door of the makeshift central office.

She waved me in, rolling her eyes and shaking her head as she did. "Don't worry about him. Been drinking all night at the back of the 7-11 on Cherry. Every once in awhile, one of the guys picks him up and takes him here, and they just let him sleep it off. Said it was better than having him go home to his girlfriend and kids like that."

Still, the feeling, that creepy crawling sensation on the back of my neck, wouldn't go away. I don't think I hallucinated the guy standing there at the doors, but it had felt like it'd been something lingering there, the end of a nightmare I'd had many times before.

"So how are you keeping her occupied?" I know I was stalling, but truthfully, I was terrified. I'd spent a good portion of my waking days and nights over the past two months researching The Square and interviewing anyone who'd been willing to come forward.

And each interviewee had been found dead inside their cars having died by carbon monoxide poisoning while running their cars in their garages not long after I'd talked to them.

Each one ruled a suicide due to absolutely no evidence of foul play.

Detective Lana Cortez and I had met during the funeral service of one of my local interview subjects. She'd approached me when I'd been helping the woman's widowed husband in the kitchen. He'd not known what to do, and her family hadn't been any help at all. In fact, they had blamed him for her death, claiming he'd not been home much to see she'd "been so unhappy with things." I think the guy was so desperate to hear from an outsider who'd had any sort of inkling as to what he was dealing with. We chatted as I arranged sandwiches on a platter while he made the coffee. Cortez just happened to catch us in the middle of our conversation when I'd mentioned The Square, and that was it for the three of us there with our suspicions, what then became our common goal. In the moment, it was just to find out more about the reach of The Square.

It didn't take long for it to become as much of an obsession for Cortez as it had for me. As soon as she set up a central office at the station, she drew the interest of a few detectives and traffic cops who'd been closely following the car collisions that had sprung up across the U.S. My own education at the Center had helped me in classifying The Square as a cult, and with Cortez now a regular presence in my world, I felt a little secure in the knowledge that we had the means to do whatever we needed to do to stop The Square from spreading any further than it already had.

The best way forward though, was to find out who the leaders were and what their end game was.

The thought of both was terrifying.

"It is so refreshing to talk to another civilian rather than another uniform." Her voice was rich with honey.

"Detective Cortez isn't in uniform though."

"It doesn't matter now, does it? She wore it plenty before she made her way up the ladder. That uniform isn't just a symbol."

"Speaking of symbols, what exactly is The Square?"

"What do you mean?"

"Well, you could've chosen something more fitting for your end result, right? Why not call yourselves Wreckers…or Crashers…or, I don't know, something over-the-top like that? The Square seems benign, out of place. I've looked into its representations, from the idea of solidity and stability… to the concept of logic…"

When Geraldine laughed, that sweet voice turned dry and dusty. "Oh, no, sweetheart, our symbolism isn't nearly so mysterious. It's a little more overt. It's just short for the 'town square'. A place for people to meet up and vent a little. But I've a feeling you've already done your research about us." She then went cold all over, leaning in. "Your auntie and uncle were believers, weren't they? Some belief system much like ours. Only differences were they kept everybody imprisoned...starved...sleepless...Not much freedom from a bunch of leaders preaching freedom, am I right?"

I should've known she'd bring it up. It didn't wholly surprise me. Nevertheless, it made my heart freeze before it thudded hard, the blood rushing in my ears.

She must have seen my jaw tighten and my ears go red because like a good cult grandma, she kept on. "When your momma died in that horrible wreck, it must've been so hard. That kind of trauma infects the soul something awful, doesn't it?"

I wasn't going to give her any more room inside of me. "What's going to happen tomorrow? What do your people have planned, Ms. Haines?"

"My people? My people will be in their homes or going about their workday, living the life they're meant to. What about your people, Mrs. Dupont? What do they have planned tomorrow? More raids on innocent citizens? More long interrogations? Not a single taxpayer around will want to hear you all are stripping good folk of their rights."

"You know I'm not with the police, Ms. Haines. You can leave any time—"

"I can?" She scoffed. "Really now!" She sipped her coffee, leaned back in her chair, and eyed me for a minute before she continued. "I guess it doesn't matter much anymore," she said with a sigh. "Keep me here or don't. Everything's like clockwork, one second at a time. How much time do you think you have, Mrs. Dupont? You and that sweet family of yours? How old's your little boy now? Six?"

The mere mention of Marbles, and I wanted to vomit. I wanted to slide across the table and throttle her.

She saw that in my posture and used it. "What is it you call him? 'Marbles'? Is that it?"

"You don't get to mention my kid. He's not part of this discussion."

"I'll bet he got that nickname from either the pastime or...." Her gaze softened as her eyes met mine. "Might be that old saying 'lost his marbles.' Something like that?"

I wasn't going to indulge her with an answer. She was partially correct, as it was when he'd heard the saying through his grandfather on Waylon's side, and then he used it whenever something went wrong. ("Don't make me lose my marbles!" he'd shout.)

"He's an adorable child," she said. "As his mother, you know perfectly well it's your duty to keep him safe from the darkness of the world. You do that plenty, don't you? Or are you too busy with your work with the Center?" She nodded slowly at me, her grin widening. "That work keeps you up at night, doesn't it? Worrying about other people's beliefs and ways..."

"I'm much more worried about the actions of such people with particular...beliefs and ways." It was my turn to slide my chair, dragging it inwards, closer to her. "So what is it you have planned? And please spare me the gaslighting and circumnavigating, especially since your...collective...has something coming tomorrow. I'd really like to know what that is. I mean, it was all over the dark web and everything..."

She cleared her throat and then made a production out of mouthing "more" and waving her empty coffee cup at the camera mounted on the ceiling. I'll give it to Cortez's precinct; they were on the ball once word got around that we had a possible leader. A rookie on duty quickly entered, completely ignoring Geraldine as he took her cup and scurried out of the room. The entire time, she'd watched him intently, probably hoping she'd catch his eye and seduce him somehow, adding him to the fold. I was proud of him for staying in control, precisely obeying what Cortez and I had ordered:

1.Absolutely no eye contact.

2.Absolutely no interaction.

Instead of responding, Geraldine waited patiently for her refill, humming a tune as she did, her hands folded on the table.

The tune she was humming, I recognized it. A lullaby.

One I used to sing to my kid when he was a baby.

I kept what little control I had left to myself, choosing instead to pinch the padding between my thumb and index finger. The pain often worked, distracting me from anyone attempting to rattle me, getting under my skin.

Geraldine though—

She was squeezing what little self-control I had left.

The rookie returned with her refill. I kept my eyes steady on her, watching her as she kept trying to meet his gaze. I couldn't take it anymore and snapped my fingers in front of her face.

"Hey! Eyes here!"

Her head whipped in my direction. I swear there was madness there, curdling. She ground her teeth together, and a thin thread of spittle hung from one corner of her mouth. She shook her head as if to clear it and wiped her mouth with the paper napkin the rookie had brought her.

"Anything else?" he mumbled at me.

"We're fine, thank you."

Once he left the room, I made a show of getting up and stretching, and then I pushed my chair up against to wall in order to stand on it and turn off the camera.

When I took the chair back and sat down again, Geraldine was watching me with a sad smile. It was more startling than the lullaby. Unnerving at any rate.

It was a look of pity.

"Ms. Haines…"

"Geraldine. Please."

"No." I wouldn't indulge her any further. "We're past pleasantries. The second you brought up my child, you changed everything between us. It's my turn."

She wilted ever so slightly. I caught it, enjoyed it. "I understand," she said softly.

"Do you?" I got up and moved my chair around so that I was able to sit right next to her, within breathing distance. "No, I don't think you do understand what it's like to devote every bit of yourself, every moment of extra time you have in the day to researching and tracking down people like you. Imagine having suffered—and I mean suffered through an entire childhood up until sixteen with people like you…like YOU…who believe we all must suffer cruelty and terror in order to reach serenity, some insane Technicolor nirvana you people concoct in your psychotic imaginations. You are a menace, a proselytizing nightmare. If I'm able to go home today, having convinced you to surrender yourself and reveal all of your reach…all of your plans…whether or not you'll be locked up for good, that's out of my hands. I'll let the authorities do that, but at least I can ease my conscience and my soul, for you will have fucking LOST, Ms. Haines. And the thought of that makes me happy. Very happy."

Geraldine went quiet, and I don't think in all my years of catching cult leaders and deprogramming followers have I ever felt so alone and scared in that moment. I wanted to know everything that would keep us all safe from the monsters of The Square.

At the same time, I wanted to know nothing.

When the silence broke, it was a roar.

"It bears repeating…We all have lost," she said. That control had resumed in her tone. "We have set about destroying ourselves since the industrial revolution, and greed was the end result, our damnation."

"What's happening tomorrow, Ms. Haines?"

"It's not what happens tomorrow, sweetheart. Tomorrow will be a new day. It's what's happening today."

"DADDY, we don't go this way to school. This is the LONG way."

Waylon glanced at his son in the rear view mirror, catching the boy's scowl, holding onto it. "We'll be okay, Mar. We'll be on time."

Marbles made a pfft-ing sound with his tongue and his lips curled around his teeth, his usual signal that he was anxious.

"It's all right, lil' man. Hey! Look out, nine o'clock!"

The boy instantly perked up, shuffling around in his seat to peer out the window. A string of horses were trotting along in a nearby pasture alongside the county road.

Just past the pasture, far off in the distance, a plume of dark smoke formed followed by another to the other side of the road beyond the valley.

"Daddy, I think there's a fire!"

"Where'd you see that?"

"Look!" He pointed in the plume's direction, the one on his side of the road.

"Probably just an accident, my guy."

Waylon caught the second and third plumes of smoke in the distance. Still, it wasn't enough to deter him from moving forward.

"TELL ME THEN, Ms. Haines. Tell me what you all have planned for today."

"But you already know, sweetheart. We're from every city… every town…every community out there that's been overpopulated to ruin. We're welcoming the next best thing to a spiritual cleansing. We're going to show you…"

WAYLON FOLLOWED the turnoff to the interstate. Then he slowed to park in the emergency lane.

"Daddy, Mom said no interstate!"

Waylon ignored his son, mounting his cell to the dash. Then he hit "record."

"Good morning," he calmly said into the camera.

"Daddy, what are you doing? Are we doing a movie?"

GERALDINE SMILED, and this time, it was warm and inviting. "We're going to show you the way, but first, we'll have to thin out the herd, just a touch."

It was then when I knew what she meant.

"I THOUGHT it was time I contributed to the great beginning here with my son," Waylon said to an invisible audience.

"What's a great beginning?"

Waylon paused for a moment to consider his next words. They would matter.

"Today is a good day, one that will be long remembered," he said. "As a member of The Square, I do this of my own free will."

He then started the car.

GERALDINE MUST HAVE SENSED my sudden awareness, read it all over my face, because she nodded knowingly at me, as if sharing a secret, as if I'd realized the revelation.

I had.

"Our loved ones across this vast country are about to become the greatest sacrifices of our time, all for the good of the earth. A renewal. Doesn't that just add the best sort of icing on the cake?"

THE DUPONTS' SUV tore through the railing of the high overpass to the interstate and went sailing before it crashed down into the traffic below, colliding with a tanker truck, setting off an explosion of fire and metal, burnt flesh and destruction.

Every major road throughout the United States was—and would continue to be throughout the cursed day—plagued with vehicular crashes. The death toll would spike from the hundreds to the thousands.

The country had officially begun to burn.

All I could think about while sitting there, paralyzed, was my husband, my kid, and when Geraldine smiled at me and said, "Your loved ones, too, sweetheart. Your loved ones, too"...

...my heart went still.

PAPE SATÀN ALEPPE

REBECCA ROWLAND

"JESUS CHRIST, Ree. Just get 'em and let's go."

Mitch wiped his hands over his face, the dirt on his palms streaking onto his reddened nose and cheeks. The temperature had grown to at least 95, if not 100, and it wasn't even noon yet.

They had been driving the backroads ever since they high tailed it out of the posh Connecticut suburb, crossing the border into Massachusetts and slinking up route 202 as it wound north under the shade of endless forest. The road had finally widened, dotted with rundown motels and convenience stores, and Irene tapped her flip-flopped foot against the floor in time with the tin can intonation of the staticky Nirvana song, stalling. Ever since Kurt Cobain had been found dead three months earlier, the radio seemed to be playing grunge music nonstop. She stared out at the side of the brick building. A white-teethed surfer girl stared back at her from a faded Newport advertisement.

Mitch had forgotten to use their code names, the pseudonyms inspired by a Steve Miller Band song they had adopted to keep their identities hidden from Sidney Plutus, Mitch's former boss's boss. Technically, he'd been the CEO of the company that employed Mitch's former boss's boss, and he was more likely to recognize their real names from randomly perusing a telephone book than he would from overhearing any of their interactions, but it was better to be safe than sorry. At least, they'd once agreed it would have been better.

"Okay, I'm going," Irene stammered, the irritation echoing in her voice. She slid out of the front seat and into the bright sunshine. As her feet made contact with the unpaved ground of the nearly empty gas station lot, small puffs of bone-dry dirt rose up like smoke signals, blanketing her toes in a fine brown spray. She hated having dirty feet and cursed herself for wearing sandals.

Irene exhaled, stuck her head back through the window, and smiled at her husband. "Anything I'm forgetting, Billy Joe?"

Mitch had begun rubbing the front of his t-shirt, his fingers leaving more dirt stains in their wake. He took a deep breath and managed to crack a smile. "No, Bobbie Sue," he said, winking. "Just don't forget the smokes." He watched her shimmy around the corner and out of sight.

They'd need gas soon, and if they were going to hop on route 2 toward the New York border, Mitch knew he better filler up now. The banging in the trunk had subsided hours earlier, and they hadn't heard a peep from ol' Sidney for at least a half an hour. Mitch guessed the guy had fallen asleep finally, or maybe passed out cold from the heat.

Out cold from the heat. Mitch snickered at that irony, then checked his reflection in the rearview mirror. He wiped half-heartedly at the grime along his forehead, the beads of sweat turning the dirt into striations of mud before seeming to absorb into the tiny lines that appeared when he raised his eyebrows. Jesus, it was hot. The air conditioner hadn't worked for years in the old Honda sedan; it was leaking freon, the mechanic had said. He'd have to replace the compressor if he wanted to fix the problem, and they didn't have the cash for such luxuries. At least, they didn't have the money a month ago. Once the payout came through, they could chuck this car and buy a brand new one.

He glanced at the gas gauge. They were at a quarter tank: that was enough fuel to make it to interstate 91, and there were certain to be stations there, but what if Sidney began his cacophony again? They couldn't risk being cornered at a pump while the old man banged and rattled the door of the trunk, making those guttural cries again. This station was nearly empty: if Sidney did try to get someone's attention, he'd be less successful than at one on the interstate.

"Pape Satàn Aleppe."

Mitch quickly turned his head, expecting to see their captive sitting in the back seat. It was Sidney Plutus' voice, but it hadn't come from the trunk. Had it? Had he imagined it?

Mitch shifted the car into reverse, backed into a semi-circle, and sidled the car next to one of the ancient gasoline pumps. If it turned out they weren't functional, it wouldn't matter much, anyway. He shut off the engine and looked toward the storefront, hoping to catch Irene's attention.

At the counter, a slim twenty-something man with greasy black hair and dirty eyeglasses stared blankly at Irene as she walked slowly up the aisle, perusing the dusty bags of chips and faded boxes of crackers. Irene shifted the two bottles of diet cola into the crook of her arm and snatched a large bag of Cheetos from the display. Mitch hated Cheetos. He'd definitely warn her, likely more than once, that she needed to be careful and not let her dirty fingers leave orange streaks on the upholstery, but she was used to that.

If they'd been in Maine, or Vermont, or, hell, any state besides Massachusetts, she'd be able to pick up a case of beer, too. Here, they'd have to shop at a packie for that, and it was too risky to make any more stops. Massachusetts was the bluest state in the country, and yet it tried to control its residents through every nit it could pick. The smokes would be pricier here, too, in goddamn Taxachusetts, she thought, and mentally rummaged through the money left in her wallet.

"Two Marlboro reds," Irene said, dropping the plastic bottles and bright orange bag onto the counter. "Hard pack, if ya got 'em." She pulled the small cotton change purse out of her back pocket and unfolded the bills stuffed inside.

The clerk blinked slowly at her and looked over at the window. "Gas, too?" he asked, jutting his chin toward the door.

Irene saw Mitch standing beside the pump, staring impatiently toward the store. She fingered the bills in her hand and glanced at the total on the register. "Yeah… twenty-five?" she asked, quickly doing the math in her head. It wouldn't fill the tank, but it would make a dent. Mitch couldn't argue: he hadn't told her they'd be getting fuel here as well.

She stepped back out into the midsummer humidity and walked quickly toward the car, the brown bag of food and cigarettes copping an awkward feel of the sweaty outline of her breasts. She maneuvered around the hood and hopped into the passenger seat, quickly unpacking the bag. As she tossed into the back seat the empty bottles from the cup holders and replaced them with the cold sodas, she eyed Mitch in the car's side mirror, who was fiddling with the pump's trigger, squeezing the last vestiges of gasoline into the tank. Coyly, she slipped the bag of Cheetos out of sight under her seat. The orange streak mansplaining could wait for an hour or two.

Irene was rhythmically knocking the top of one of the boxes of Marlboros against her left hand as Mitch opened the driver's side door and slumped heavily into the seat. His face glistened with a wet brownish sheen.

"Drink something," Irene said, pausing in her tobacco packing ritual to point toward the bottles already drenched with condensation. "You're gonna be sick otherwise."

He did as he was told, nearly finishing half of the 20 ounces in a single gulp, and Irene let her gaze wander down her husband's doughy body as his Adam's apple bobbed behind black stubble. They'd been married for five years. Five years seemed like a long time to Irene, who'd walked down the aisle just two weeks after collecting her high school diploma. Mitch was older than her—ten years older—and had promised his new bride that the entry level position as a security guard for Frost Pharmaceuticals was just that: an entrance. It was the running start that would propel him up and into a lucrative position within the fast-growing drug powerhouse before they bounced their first kid.

Five years later, there were no kids, but that was just as well: there wasn't an expensive suit-clad knee to bounce one on, either. Mitch's career had wallowed in place before he was fired five months earlier, on Valentine's Day. At least that's when he'd swallowed enough liquid courage to tell her. She was too busy scrubbing the Jim Beam-scented vomit stains from the toilet rim the next day to question him further. Once he'd proposed the plan to hold Sidney for ransom, her curiosity became otherwise distracted.

Mitch screwed the cap back on the bottle and handed it to Irene. "I'm exhausted," he said, turning the key. The engine hummed to life. "I've been up for twenty-seven hours. Why don't we get a motel room—something cheap, you know, like one of those rundown hooker shacks in the middle of nowhere—and I'll take a quick nap and we can boogie." He pulled his seatbelt across his torso, clicked the catch, and shifted the gear into Drive.

Irene placed the bottle between her knees. Its cool wetness felt lovely on her hot skin. "If it's just a nap, why don't we pull over at one of those rest stops? Or maybe—" She pulled the wrinkled map from the door jam and scanned it, trying to determine their location. "Yeah, there's a park a few miles up the route in Orange. And a campground less than a hour away in…" She squinted at the text. "… Erving? Why don't we just go there, park in the shade, try to catch an hour of sleep before grabbing a meal closer to the border?" Irene waited for her husband to pull the car back into traffic and turn onto the onramp. "I'm down to twenty-six dollars, Billy Joe," she added. "I'd rather spend money on a full night's sleep, you know?"

Mitch couldn't argue with that. They drove west in relative silence, all of the windows rolled down so that the highway speed's wind might blow the sweat from their skin and clothes. When they reached the entrance to the Wagon Wheel Campground, Irene unwrapped the first pack of Marlboros. She pushed her disheveled hair from her face and shoved two in her mouth, one for each of them, then patted her shorts pockets, trying to recover the lighter to set them alight.

It wasn't until she blew out the first stream of smoke from her mouth and took one of the cigarettes from her lips to offer to her husband that she noticed he hadn't moved the car from their spot fifty yards or so from the gate. "What's wrong?" she asked.

Mitch accepted the cigarette and used it to point at a spot in the distance. "Wagon Wheel is a horse camp. We can't rent a space here. Too conspicuous."

"Conspicuous?" Irene echoed. "Why?"

"Did you pack a fucking horse that I don't know about?" Mitch replied angrily. It came out much more sharply than he intended, and he knew it was the exhaustion talking, but somehow, he couldn't bring himself to apologize. He took a long drag and tapped the steering wheel with his other hand.

Irene searched the map again. "'Looks like there's a state park right next door. Let's just head there, park in the lot. It's barely noon. We can set the alarm, sleep until dinner."

Mitch exhaled a long stream of white smoke. "Okay," he said finally. "Which way from here?"

The lot was nearly full in Erving State Park, the three only available spaces sizzling smack in the middle of the scorching blacktop. Mitch pulled into the middle spot, leaving an empty space on either side of them. The both climbed out of the car and looked around. There was a small lake nearby and a sandy beach teeming with visitors. Irene glanced at the sky. It was a perfect, peaceful blue, without even a whisper of cloud in sight. The bright yellow sun, naked without a stitch of self-consciousness, bore down on them like a ravenous hunting dog leaping at its prey.

Mitch held a hand to his forehead like a visor. "I'm going to jump in the water, then lay out in the back there," he nodded his head, "under the trees. You with me?"

Irene glanced toward the trunk. "Should we check on..." She didn't want to say his name, afraid she'd jinx the silence they'd enjoyed from their captured collateral for the past two hours. She'd almost forgotten why they were traveling.

Mitch reached into the back seat and pulled a blanket from the duffle bag they'd stored there. "Yeah, yeah. Give me a second. Roll up the windows most of the way, but keep them cracked. Throw a t-shirt or something over the steering wheel, would ya? Just so I don't burn my palms off when we get back in."

As Irene climbed back into the front seat, reaching toward the bag to find the item he'd requested, Mitch shoved a fresh cigarette in his mouth and the blanket over one shoulder, then walked to the back of the car. He took a deep breath and steeled his legs. His jaw still ached where Plutus had popped him one the night before. He wasn't about to let his guard down again. After a minute, he stuck the key in the trunk latch and turned it until a barely audible click sounded.

Irene climbed back out of the car wearing her sunglasses. Her ragged Old Orchard Beach t-shirt barely covered the steering wheel, but it would have to do. "Everything okay?" she stage whispered.

Mitch shut the trunk and walked toward her, his face expressionless. "Yep. He's out like a light," he said. "Stinks to high heaven, too. If you think I smell bad after sweating all day in the car, honey, you should take a whiff of ol' Sidney. 'Might have shit himself, I think."

Irene wrinkled her nose. "Well, that's not good," she responded, unsure of what to say next.

Mitch shrugged. "I'm not worrying about it now. Let's go take a dip."

IT SEEMED LIKE A FOOLPROOF PLAN. Mitch had been to Sidney Plutus's house exactly one time, long before she and Mitch had married: it was a company Christmas party he somehow had finagled an invitation to in the hopes of networking with some of the executives. Although the company headquarters nested near the Southern edge of the state, the Plutus home—mansion, more like it, according to Mitch—was closer to the state capital, on the northern side. Strangely enough, it wasn't in a gated community, and he didn't employ much security. On the rare occasion that an alarm was tripped at the house when its owner was not at home, one of the senior guards at the headquarters was sent to meet with the police. Mitch had known about these incidences, but he'd never been assigned house duty.

He also knew that the last weekend of every month, Sidney took a red eye to San Francisco. Rumor had it that he kept a family, or maybe just a secret lover, on the West Coast, but only the security department had been made aware of this routine. Still, the CEO never employed one of the guards, or even a car service, to drive him to Bradley International Airport; the man preferred to drive himself.

"Control freak." Mitch mumbled this under his breath as the two of them watched the garage door open and the silver Mercedes slide almost silently from its depths and onto the driveway. "And three, two, one..." As if on cue, the luxury car's engine cut off. The car rolled forward a few inches, then bluntly stopped.

"How did you—" Irene began, forgetting to keep her voice low.

"Shhhh!" Mitch cut her off. He did not take his eyes off the car as he reminded her. "As soon as you see me reach the car, pull it all the way up. Don't turn on the headlights, whatever you do. Okay?"

He had opened the door without her noticing, the interior lights having been switched off in preparation for their operation. Before she could respond, he was padding up the dark driveway, toward Sidney, who had exited his stalled vehicle in confusion. Before she knew it, Mitch was standing in front of the CEO, then had his hands around his neck. Irene pressed her foot on the gas and zipped the Honda over to the pair, pulling the trunk release latch as she stepped on the brake and ground the shifter into Park. She and Mitch lumbered toward the trunk simultaneously, him half-escorting, half-dragging a stunned Sidney Plutus alongside.

"What the fuck do you think you're doing?" the man gasped menacingly. "Do you know who I am?"

Irene pushed the trunk door open. They'd forgotten to disable the light there, and she pawed frantically at the wires, finally resorting to ripping the bulb from its tether. Mitch shoved Sidney into the trunk, slamming the back of the old man's head into one of the giant metal prongs of the jumper cables they kept there.

"Yeah, I know," replied Mitch. He leaned down to push the man's shoulders against the floor while Irene pulled a small length of duct tape from a roll. Before she could bind his wrists, Sidney punched Mitch in the jaw with a closed fist, stunning him for a second.

"Pape Satàn," said Sidney. "Pape Satàn, Aleppe!" In the cool glow of moonlight, his eyes danced wildly. He grinned like a madman and strangely, did not make an attempt to escape.

"Shut. The fuck. Up," said Mitch, seemingly unfazed by the man's response. He pulled an old washcloth from his pocket and shoved it between Sidney's lips, then grabbed the strip of duct tape from Irene's hand and slapped it over his mouth. "Tear off a new strip," he hissed at his wife. "Quick. To bind his arms."

Irene stood frozen in place. Was this déjà vu? Hadn't this happened just the night before? What were they doing? She began fiddling with the silver roll in her hand when she felt a hand shake her shoulder. She turned in confusion, unsure how Mitch could be shaking her when both of his hands were clamped firmly on Sidney's wrists, holding him down. She turned to see a tall boy, his face sprinkled with acne, wearing only faded green swim trunks, holding her upper arm.

They weren't in Sidney's driveway; they were on the blanket on the lake's shore, under a broad pine tree. Above them, the sky was cerulean blue, orange and pink encircling the sun in the distant horizon. They had overslept. "Oh...oh...I'm sorry..." she stammered. "We—we must have fallen asleep." Mitch was dozing on the blanket next to her and she shook him violently.

"Sorry: beach is closed for the night," the tall boy said robotically. It was clear it was something he said on a daily basis as he swept the sand for vagrants and irresponsible parents at the end of each minimum-wage shift.

Mitch awoke with a start and sat up. "What time is it? Jesus... Jesus..." He put his t-shirt back on and hopped to his feet, looking at the sky. "What is it? Eight o'clock?"

The boy crossed his arms over his skinny, hairless chest. "Seven-fifteen. Beach closes at seven."

Irene stood up and grabbed the blanket, folding it awkwardly over her arm. She felt like a teenager who'd been caught humping her boyfriend in the bathroom of a department store. "We're sorry. We're going." Mitch was already walking toward the lot, and she struggled to catch up to him in her flip-flops over the malleable sand.

Their black sedan was the only car in sight, but Mitch stood at the edge of the lot, hesitating. "What's the matter?" Irene asked when she reached his side.

"Shhhh," Mitch whispered. "Shit. I wish I had a bat, or a tennis racket or something." He put his hands on his hips. Irene followed his gaze. There, at the back of their car, stood a family of large raccoons—at least five or six in number, half of them stretched onto their hind legs and pressing their noses against the trunk. A few pointed their snouts at the sky and bobbed their heads as if sniffing the air but then quickly returned their attention to the car. One looked directly at Irene and Mitch and hissed.

"Why are there so many?" Irene whispered. "Do you think they're rabid?"

Mitch's expression turned slightly sick at this question. He hadn't considered that the animals might turn aggressive. He just wanted them away from the car before their congregation attracted the attention of the beach patrol boy, or even worse, an adult park employee. "You got the smokes?" he asked, shifting his weight from foot to foot. His stomach growled. They hadn't eaten anything since their hasty fast food breakfast at sunrise, Mitch parked two lots away while Irene ran down the street and into the takeout line,

Sidney Plutus moaning and banging his body against the bowels of the car's storage compartment the whole time.

Irene lit a cigarette and passed it to her husband. "What are we going to do?" she asked. "How are—"

Suddenly, Mitch let out a ferocious yell, an incoherent primal scream, and began running toward the car, waving his arms in disorganized frustration. A small puff of white cigarette smoke trailed behind him, making him appear like an intoxicated dragon. The creatures froze, then one—the likely alpha of the group—took two tiny steps forward as if to defend the pack's new territory, but Irene felt her shoulders relax in relief when it and the rest of the raccoons returned to all-fours and shuffled quickly away, into the dark shelter of the woods.

When Mitch reached the car, he stopped and bent over, resting his hands on his knees. "I'm winded and I only ran like fifty feet."

Irene walked to the back of the car. "What did they smell, do you think?" She stared at the trunk's hood. "'You think he's awake yet? Maybe he made a noise to call them over?"

Mitch straightened himself up. "Nah. Don't worry about it," he said. "Get in the car. Let's get something to eat. I'm sure there's a pub nearby that serves food until close." He walked to the driver's side and unlocked the door.

"Open the trunk." Irene did not move. Something was nagging at the back of her brain. "I'm serious. Pull the latch."

Mitch opened his door. "Ree, come on. We'll deal with him later..." He tilted his head to the side like he always did when he was too tired to argue.

"No." The firmness in her voice surprised even her. "Unlock it."

Mitch walked toward her with the keys in his hand. He unlocked the latch and the trunk door bobbed open. A putrid stench rose from the opening, knocking Irene backward. She covered her nose and mouth with one hand. "Oh, god: you weren't kidding." She held her nose closed with her finger and thumb and exhaled through her mouth.

Without acknowledging her, Mitch grabbed the lip of the door and pulled the trunk open completely. The stink rose with it, wafting over Irene and Mitch like a rotting blanket: a combination of feces, spoiled meat, and overripe cheese, choking their lungs.

Irene looked inside the trunk and quickly moved her hand to her eyes. "Oh my god," she moaned. "Oh, no: Mitch, is he, is he..."

Mitch motioned with his hand to keep her voice down. "Shhh... yes. He probably died somewhere between the state border and the gas station. Heat exhaustion, my guess." His voice was eerily flat.

Irene looked at her husband incredulously. "You knew? When were you going to tell me?"

Mitch scratched his head. "I suspected, maybe. You know, when he didn't move or anything when we got here. And then...I guess I was just so tired, and we couldn't do anything if he was dead, so—"

"So you just went for a fucking swim?!" Irene forgot to be horrified, her disbelief quickly replaced with anger. "We have a dead man in our car trunk. No one is going to pay a ransom now. What are we going to do?"

Mitch flicked an ash onto the pavement. "Look: the good news is, no one is looking for us. We didn't call with the money demand. If we just dump him, clean up the trunk, drive back home, no one will be the wiser. Besides," he took a final drag on his cigarette and tossed the butt onto the ground. "There's bound to be a reward for information leading to his body being recovered. We'll say we were on vacation up here, then 'accidentally' discover him, call the police, and poof: we're heroes."

"Are you high?" Irene stared at Mitch, unblinking. "You have got to be kidding me." She allowed her eyes to return to the body in the trunk. Sidney Plutus' eyes were open but slightly hooded, as if he were tired, the round pupils swallowing most of the gray of his irises. A pale brown substance was caked on the side of his mouth: vomit, or perhaps blood-tinged saliva dried to a crust. He lay slightly on his right side, his knees curled up like a child, the way Irene sometimes slept. She reached out and placed her hand hesitantly on his shoulder.

"Don't touch him," Mitch said, but Irene ignored him. She

pushed slightly on Sidney's shoulder and the old man tipped backwards. To her horror, Irene saw that the entire side of Sidney's face as well as his upper arm, the parts touching the floor of the cabin, were a deep violet-red, nearly black. A fresh wave of retching miasma wafted upwards. Where the man's body had lain, a dark, wet outline remained.

"Why are his legs like that?" Irene asked, no longer covering her face but concentrating instead on inhaling slowly through her mouth to keep from vomiting. Although Sidney lay on his back, his knees remained rigidly bent, as if he'd been caught participating in a strange game of Twister. The skin of one ankle, peeking out from an unsocked loafer, was bloated and dark purple—shiny and wet like the skin of a ripe plum.

"You watch Forensic Files. Rigor mortis would be my guess," said Mitch. He leaned down close to the man's face. "I guess all those painkillers Frost is pushing won't do you no good now, huh, Sid?"

Irene pulled him back. "Stop it."

Mitch acquiesced and walked around to the driver's side door. "Are you coming? I'm starving."

"Yeah." Irene raised her arm and gripped the edge of the lid, keeping her gaze fixed on the corpse lying face-up in front of her. As the trunk lowered, Irene swore that in her final view of the compartment, she saw Sidney's eyes roll toward her and his mouth contort into a terrible grin.

"I'm Sam," said the bartender at the Rendezvous in a voice that was neither irritated nor particularly welcoming. "Let me know what I can get for you."

"Thanks," said Irene. Sam turned and addressed another customer further down the bar. Mitch scanned the laminated menu, then glanced up at the chalkboard with handwritten selections of the beers on tap. Below the board, a small television with a cable box balancing atop played music videos.

"Serves him right," Mitch said finally. "You know? He was running a company that might as well be a factory for addiction centers. They are pushing out new opioids like they're Tic Tacs. Do you know how many heroin addicts will have him to thank in five years?"

Irene sniffed. "And you wanted to be a big wig in that addiction factory. We wanted to siphon the profit from that addiction factory."

Mitch turned his body to face her. "He deserved it!"

"We weren't going to donate the ransom to drug treatment centers, were we?" Irene smirked. "We're just as bad as him. Except, unlike him, we're probably going to jail." They were both quiet for a moment. On the television, Bjork ran through a dark forest, a giant teddy bear following menacingly behind. "I still don't understand what he was saying. Papa, Satan, Aleppo? What does that even mean?"

Mitch rolled his eyes. "Does it matter?" He slid off the barstool. "I'm going to the bathroom. Order me an IPA, okay, Bobbie Sue?" He sighed and walked toward a sign at the rear of the room marked Men's with an arrow.

"What are you studying?" Sam reappeared. He was a pale, thin man with hair tied back into a short ponytail. He wiped the space on the bar in front of Irene and placed a fresh coaster in front of her.

"What?" Irene blushed. She'd never been mistaken for a college student before. She certainly looked young enough to still be in school, but somehow, no one ever lumped her in with the pretty co-eds that sometimes dotted the coffee shop or dive bar near their apartment. "I'm not—"

"Sorry. I overheard a snippet of what you were saying. Pape Satàn, Aleppe, right?" said the bartender. "Lit class or Classics?" He didn't pause for her response. "I remember thinking, yeah, it would be so cool to read The Inferno. And then I got to it, and I was like, Thanks for stuffing this with inside jokes and figures only relevant to the fourteenth century, Dante." He tucked the end of the rag into his belt. "Pape Satàn Aleppe. From the fourth circle of hell. I remember that one because we spent so much time debating what it meant."

Irene held her breath and tried to keep her expression neutral. "What do you think it means?"

Sam thought for a moment. "Well...it's the God of Wealth that is standing at the gate of the circle, yelling this at Dante and Virgil, right? Most people think it's an invocation to Lucifer, like, this guy is trying to ward off trespassers by threatening to expose them to even greater evils of hell if they continue. But they are already in hell, so what's the threat, really?"

Mitch returned to the bar and sat back in his stool but said nothing. He turned his eyes to the television set. The giant teddy bear began to beat on a man dressed as a lumberjack then dragged his limp body away.

Irene cleared her throat. "If it's not a warning, what did he mean?"

The bartender smiled. It was clear he enjoyed revisiting his long lost school years. Irene glanced quickly at the other patrons: they were mostly twenty-somethings, dressed in hipster fashion and sipping craft beers. "I think," Sam said, "he wasn't invoking Lucifer to come. I think he was greeting Lucifer, as if Dante himself were the Prince of Darkness. Not literally, but maybe as a way to say, we all have the potential for evil. Especially in that fourth circle, right? That's the circle for greed. We all go a little avaricious sometimes, yeah?" A nearby customer called for his attention, and Sam held one finger up. "Anyway," he added, "besides Virgil and Dante, everyone there was already in hell. They were getting the punishments they deserved, at least according to Dante."

The customer called Sam's name again and the bartender excused himself. "Did you order my beer?" asked Mitch. He picked up the menu again. "I could go for a cheeseburger. Maybe the pulled pork sandwich."

Irene pushed her stool away from the bar. "I'm going out for a smoke, Billy Joe." She lifted the keys from his front pocket, then patted her shorts pockets, only then realizing they were empty. "I left them in the car. Order me something. I don't care what." She smoothed the back of her hair and walked outside.

The air was still heavy, a thick wool blanket smothering the earth, even though it was nearly nine in the evening. Irene unlocked the passenger side door and grabbed the red box from the center console. There was only one cigarette left, and she threw the empty container in the back seat and closed the door. She walked to the back of the car and leaned against the trunk, taking a deep drag.

In two weeks, it would be August. Mitch's unemployment would run out soon. She had asked him to try applying for other security positions: they always needed people at the bank, or maybe even at the mall or the college. He'd been at Frost for more than half a decade: surely they'd provide a decent reference, even if they let him go for chronic tardiness or perhaps not working as hard as they had liked. Mitch shot her down, though. He weaseled out of the topic each time she brought it up. They'd assumed any money they had to spend on this trip would be replaced ten-fold—hell, hundred-fold—when the ransom was paid. Now, they'd be using some of their August rent for dinner and a night in a cheap motel.

She bit the nail on the thumb of the hand holding the cigarette and considered this, then jumped forward on reflex. Something in the car had moved: she was sure of it, a slight vibration pushing against the back of her thigh. She examined the trunk's lid, then the latch. Nothing seemed out of order. Even the taillights were pristine. She remembered wistfully how she and a friend in junior high had taken turns locking each other in the trunk of her mother's Monte Carlo. They'd watched a talk show—Donahue or Sally Jesse, or maybe even that guy with the mustache who did a special on Al Capone's vault—on how to survive an abduction. You never knew when a random cult member might pluck you off the streets on your way home from school and shove you in the car trunk to be taken god-knows-where. According to the show's expert, you were supposed to kick the taillight, break the plastic if possible. That would alert law enforcement to pull the car over for a citation, and then, when the cops were in earshot, you were supposed to scream like the dickens.

Apparently, Sidney hadn't seen that show.

She leaned against the trunk again, taking a final drag before dropping the butt on the dirt and stomping it out with her sandal. Despite the early afternoon swim, her feet were still filthy, she noted with some dismay. It would be nice to finally take a shower at the motel, no matter what it cost them.

You were supposed to pull on the wires.

It came to her, the other important tip they'd learned from the show. If you didn't kick the taillight hard enough to break it, you were supposed to damage the wires leading to the light in some way. If you caused a short, they might blink, or they might go out altogether. Either way, it was another way of luring help before you were whisked off to become someone's offering to the devil.

The old man had thrashed about quite a bit when they'd initially been driving. He'd banged around for hours: that had been the primary reason they'd taken the back roads, to avoid as many other cars and people as possible. Had he managed to damage one of their lights?

Irene opened the driver's side door and leaned in. She stuck the key in the ignition and turned it forward just a hair, enough to make the dashboard come to life and the irritating alarm ding to warn her that a door was ajar. She turned on the headlights, then shut the door and walked behind the car again.

All four lights glowed in unison, two red and two white. The lower right one, the white directional, blinked slightly. Irene reassured herself, it was just a trick on her tired eyes. She looked away, then focused on the parking lamp again. It stayed lit…then, sure enough, it went dark for a beat, then lit again.

Irene leaned forward and knocked lightly on the lamp. The beam shivered a bit, a quick strobe. A short, Irene thought. There's a short in the wire. She had to find a way to fix it. Whether Sidney had damaged it or not, it might attract the attention of a squad car. She knew the police couldn't randomly search vehicles without a warrant, but the smell...she wondered if soon, other people would be able to smell what was in the trunk. The stench of decay might warrant just cause.

Irene retrieved the keys from the ignition and turned off the lights. She inserted the key in the trunk's lock and hesitated, preparing herself for Sidney's upturned face again. The dead eyes, staring blankly at the sky. The blood pooled on one side of his body, primed to burst from his skin at any moment.

She took a deep breath and pushed open the lid.

Sidney wasn't lying on his back. He had turned over onto his other side and was facing the back of the compartment. One of his arms was out of sight, and the other lay limply along his hip. Swathes of bloated purple stretched everywhere skin was visible. The scent of rotting flesh had intensified, and Irene could see two houseflies circling his face.

Something was wrong. Something had changed, it was—

Why weren't Sidney's wrists bound?

She grasped the edge of the lid to shut the door when Sidney turned over again. His eyes stayed rooted in place, staring blindly forward even as his hands shot out and pulled Irene on top of him. She began to scream, but the sound was quickly cut short when the old man clamped a distended purple hand over her mouth and shoved the putrid, wet rag that had been in his throat into hers.

I'm dreaming again. I'm dreaming. Irene told herself, squeezing her eyes tightly shut and wriggling like mad to slip free from the dead man's grasp. She would wake up any moment now. She would wake up and they'd be back on the blanket at the lake, or maybe—even better—in her own bed, at home.

"Pape Satàn, Aleppe," Sidney growled into her ear, the words thick and wet in his decaying throat. "Do you know who I am? Better yet, do you know where you are?"

And with that, the car's trunk slammed shut, enveloping Irene in darkness.

THE STONE COLLECTOR

SONORA TAYLOR

LAVINIA'S HOME was not as fancy as her name. She lived with her mother and sister, Penelope, in a worn-down cottage on the outskirts of their village. They hadn't been banished, her mother simply liked the solitude. "The forest makes you strong," her mother said as Penelope clutched for dear life to her mother's shift, sucking her exposed breast as her mother stirred a mushroom and venison stew for their supper. "Everything in this house came from the woods. We don't need anything more. We have just enough."

Lavinia disagreed. Whenever she and her mother went into town to sell crystals and jewelry they spent their days making, Lavinia marveled at what everyone had. The women wore dresses with beautiful colors, cloaks that kept away the cold wind and caught the sunlight in their golden threads. Families led fat cows and large pigs through the square, animals with far more meat to spare for her mother's stew pot. Vendors sold vegetables and fruit that Lavinia could never find in the woods, and others still sold sugary sweets that Lavinia would give anything to taste.

But even when their wares sold well, her mother wouldn't let her buy the things she wanted. "This money is for what we need," her mother said as their cart became laden with scratchy, ugly swaths of linen and wool, no satin or color to be found. Sweets, vegetables, and animals were left behind altogether. "The forest will provide," her mother said as they walked towards their cottage at sundown.

Lavinia sighed as she stared at the array of trees, paths, and boulders behind their cottage. She wished it would provide more.

LAVINIA'S primary chore was to find stones her mother could polish into gems for their jewelry. After her twelfth birthday, her mother let her go into the woods alone. "Watch out for holes and roots," she'd always call as Lavinia left with an empty sack, one that weighed on her back to tell her when she'd collected enough.

One morning, a couple days before market, Lavinia left after breakfast to complete her chore. It was a cloudy day, but the morning dew on the grass told her it wouldn't rain. That didn't make the stray blades of grass nor the muddied clumps of dirt any less irritating upon her bare feet. She searched for smooth stones that could be polished, namely colorful crystals her mother could make into beautiful gems. No matter the quality of the rock, Lavinia added them to her bag with a frown on her face. If we were rich like our customers, I wouldn't be in these woods digging through the dirt to get materials that help us barely scrape by, she thought as she threw a rock into her sack.

An acorn fell with a strong thunk on her head. Lavinia cursed, her words echoing across the forest floor. She rubbed her head and looked up. Her hand froze. An empty cave she'd never noticed stood before her in the distance.

Lavinia would've turned away, but a tiny glint caught her attention. It shimmered from the mouth of the cave. Is that a diamond? she wondered. Holding her sack that was still too light to take to her mother, she made her way towards the cave.

Darkness greeted her when she arrived. Lavinia hesitated outside the mouth of the cave. Were there bears inside?

"You can come in."

The whisper called inside her mind, but Lavinia knew it wasn't her own thought. She shuddered and took a step back.

"Don't be afraid," the whisper added. Before Lavinia could turn and run, she saw two shimmers where there had been one. Then three, then four, until a carpet of stars seemed to twinkle on the cave floor. Lavinia thought of the jewelry her mother could make—and maybe perhaps, the stones she could keep for herself.

Lavinia walked inside. The glittering lights snuffed out, and darkness surrounded her. Lavinia turned and could no longer see the opening of the cave.

"Focus ..." The whisper moved through the cave like a breath.

"Where am I?" Lavinia asked.

"Within your desires."

"Who are you?"

"What do you want?"

Lavinia backed away and hit a stone wall. She turned and smacked against another. She felt walls against her toes and the coolness of stone breathe onto her back. "Let me out!" she screamed.

"Tell me what you want!" The voice remained a whisper, but it tore through Lavinia's ears.

"The stones!" she cried. "To make jewelry."

"That is a need. What do you want?"

The walls pressed Lavinia on all four sides. "I want to get out!"

"That too is a need." The cave walls squeezed her more tightly still. All this because she'd wanted what she thought was a diamond.

That diamond. That glimmer. That want.

"Diamonds!" Lavinia cried. "My own jewelry. Beautiful clothes lined with jewels."

Lavinia's body was released. Sunlight came from the mouth of the cave. At her feet stood a small pile of grey stones.

"Take them," the whisper instructed.

Lavinia furrowed her brow. "They're rocks."

"Take them."

Lavinia wanted nothing more than to leave the cave. Afraid to ignore the whisper's commands, she threw the stones into her sack and ran away.

"LAVINIA! WHAT'S THE MATTER?"

Her mother watched in shock as Lavinia dashed into their cottage and slammed the door. Lavinia couldn't answer until she caught her breath.

"Did you see a bear?" Her mother glanced at the sack on the floor. "Is that why your sack's so bare?"

"A cave ..." Lavinia managed to pant.

"Well what'd you go into a cave for? Right into a mother bear's den."

"No bear ... stones ..."

"No stone is worth a bear chasing you from your chores." Her mother huffed as she picked up the sack. "Especially ones that only leave your bag half full."

Lavinia gritted her teeth. If her mother cared so much about how many stones they had, then why did they live in squalor on the outskirts of town? They had everything they needed, so long as Lavinia was the only one providing.

Lavinia kept her grievances to herself, simply replying, "I'll get more."

But her mother's face was no longer angry. "No need," she said with a smile. "Why didn't you tell me what you got?"

Lavinia furrowed her brow. "What do you mean?"

Her mother reached into the sack and lifted out a handful of glittering moonstones. Lavinia's mouth dropped. "These are precious crystals!" her mother said. "And look." She dropped the moonstone back in the bag and lifted out two gold nuggets. "We can use the gold to cast it. We'll make a fortune from these!"

Lavinia couldn't believe it. The stones she'd gathered in haste from the cave were grey and dull. Stones you'd find anywhere.

But she hadn't found them just anywhere—she'd found them in a mysterious cave. One that seemed to know exactly what she wanted.

THE JEWELRY LAVINIA and her mother crafted from the stones in the cave were some of their most beautiful works. Patrons new and regular fawned over the wares at the market that week. "We'll be doing well this week," her mother said with a smile as they made their way back to their shack with the ever-rare empty cart of wares.

Lavinia merely shrugged. None of the jewelry had been saved for her, and her mother hadn't allowed her to take any of the money to buy something from one of the neighboring vendors.

Her mother glanced over her shoulder at Lavinia, then lost her smile. "What's got you sporting such a sour puss?" she asked.

"I wanted to buy something else at the market. We made enough."

"We need this money for necessities—"

"We had enough."

"What with the baby and all—"

"The baby sucks your breast and sleeps in a crib! What more could she need?"

Her mother raised a hand and Lavinia flinched, bracing for impact. However, her mother lowered her arm before striking a blow. "You should learn gratitude," she muttered, before turning back towards the cottage.

Lavinia swallowed the wad of saliva she wished to spit on the ground. What did her mother know about gratitude? Lavinia had nearly been crushed to death by a cave to bring back a sack of beautiful stones, and all she got in return was the same things they always had: just enough money for provisions, a shoddy cottage, and a baby that only stopped crying when she shat.

"Come along inside," her mother called. "I'm making venison stew."

Lavinia's stomach growled, and she picked up her step.

THE NEXT MORNING, when Lavinia's mother tossed the empty stone collecting sack in Lavinia's direction, she didn't grab it with her usual eye roll. She darted out the door and sped towards the woods. The sparkle of dew on the grass reminded Lavinia of the riches to come when she found the cave.

Once she reached the woods, Lavinia slowed her step. She walked in the direction of the cave as best as she could remember it. Her pace slowed more as she went further and deeper into the forest. Where had she spotted the cave? It was hard to remember, for it had caught her eye when she'd been walking.

A glint shimmered in her periphery. Lavinia smiled and turned to her left. The cave stood waiting. Its cavern was dark, but Lavinia knew that shiny wonders waited inside. She approached the cave and saw several grey stones piled towards the front.

Lavinia looked into the darkness. She shuddered at the memory of the cave's walls closing in on her, as well as the mysterious whisper. She knelt to the ground just outside of the cave and picked up one stone. No whisper. She gathered two more. Nothing.

Lavinia sighed with relief. She could get the stones and not have to encounter what lay inside. She filled her sack until it was twice as full as the day before, then made her way back home. She thought she felt a cold breath encircle her ankles as she left the cave, but she figured it was just the breeze.

"Back already?" her mother said when Lavinia walked inside. She sat at the table cutting cords for necklaces, while Penelope slept in her cradle in a rare moment of silence.

"I brought more of the stones I found last time," Lavinia said as she heaved the sack onto the table.

"Watch my cords!"

"We'll be able to make even more of those beautiful pieces the women at the market loved so much."

Her mother finally smiled, then stood and peered into the sack. Her smile quickly vanished. "Are you joking?"

Lavinia peered inside the bag. Her jaw dropped. It was filled with round, grey stones—just like she'd collected. No moonstones, no gold, nothing special.

"What are you doing bringing these rocks back?" her mother asked.

"They're the same ones I brought before."

"You know I send you to find crystals and gems."

"Maybe they need a moment to change."

"Change?" Her mother laughed, and it sounded like she was spitting. Lavinia felt as if her heart were hit with the phlegm. "You're daft, girl. I hope your sister grows up less mad than you!"

"These were the same rocks I got yesterday," Lavinia insisted, though in a quieter voice. Her cheeks were flushed and her throat was tight.

"And I'm the bloody queen." Her mother shoved the sack back towards Lavinia. "Take this back and get something we can use. And don't come back until you do."

Lavinia took the sack and left the cottage in a huff, dumping the useless stones in the grass before heading back towards the woods. She raced along the path, the woods growing deeper and her temper growing stronger with each step. Though she moved more quickly than she had that morning, it still took her longer to find the cave—which only deepened her anger. "Where are you?" she shouted into the trees.

One glimmer, then two, caught her eye. Lavinia scoffed as she turned to face the cave. "Coming on command, then?" she asked as she moved towards the cave.

"Only yours."

Lavinia froze. That whisper again. She softened, but in fear as opposed to any sense of calm. "Why didn't the stones change?" she asked.

"You didn't say what you wanted."

"I wanted the stones." Lavinia shivered at the memory of the cave's walls closing in on her. "I wanted the same things I asked for before."

"You must want more."

Lavinia frowned. "I want more stones."

"Come inside."

She smiled. It was easier than she thought. She trotted inside the cave, and didn't even flinch when the light of the woods behind her snuffed out like a candle. She dropped to her knees and felt around on the floor for stones. Every surface and corner, though, was smooth and cold to the touch.

"Are you all out?" she asked.

A sigh sounded around her. It flowed in a continuous stream that cooled the cave yet burned Lavinia's ears. She rose to her feet.

"What do you want?" the whisper asked.

Several short, cold tendrils snatched her ankles. Lavinia gasped, then knelt to bat them away. More tendrils grabbed her wrists and yanked her back against the cave's walls. They wrapped around her wrists and ankles so tightly that only Lavinia's pulse could move against them.

"What do you want?" the whisper asked again.

"I want you to let me go!" Lavinia shrieked as a longer tendril snaked its way around her waist. The cave was so dark that she couldn't see what held her captive. Were they ropes? Vines? Lavinia heard a hiss and stiffened with a start. "Don't let them bite me!"

The hiss became a chuckle, and Lavinia realized that snakes weren't her captor—only the cave. "What do you want?"

"Money. Riches. Beautiful clothes." All of the tendrils squeezed Lavinia tightly, and she added, "My own money. My own wares. Something my mother can't snatch away for her shack or her crafts or to spoil my sister!"

The tendrils loosened, and Lavinia sighed.

"What will you give?" the whisper asked.

Lavinia paused. Give?

"What will you give?"

The tendrils tightened, and Lavinia shrieked. "Money!" she said.

"You want money for yourself."

"I can give you some of it."

"I don't want what you want. Your desires have already created the stones."

Lavinia heard a small avalanche tumble to the cave's floor. Despite her circumstances, her mouth almost watered at the thought of all the gems she'd have in her sack. But there was no getting to the sack if she was bound to the cave's wall—and the tendrils had not loosened their grip.

"Then why won't you let me go?"

"Because I need more than what you crave."

"What do you need?"

A gentle hum began to crescendo in Lavinia's ears. They both began to burn. The flush moved from her cheeks to her fingertips. Her wrists and ankles throbbed harder against the tendrils.

"Something to warm my veins," the whisper purred.

Lavinia's skin went cold. Did the cave want her blood?

The tendrils squeezed more tightly. In a panic, she bit her lip until it began to bleed. She then bent forward so the blood could drip on the tendrils. She only hoped her aim was correct.

Her left hand was freed, and then her right. She spat more blood onto her palms and rubbed the tendrils on her waist and ankles, each freeing her one-by-one.

Light poured into the cave. The entrance was back. Near it lay mountains of stones—ones that Lavinia knew would transform when she brought them home.

Lavinia was covered in sweat by the time she arrived at the cottage, but she didn't care. Her mother's smile when she opened the sack told Lavinia that the episode with the tendrils in the cave had all been worth it.

"You've found a mine!" her mother exclaimed as she lifted some of the contents into the air. Lavinia's mouth dropped. Her mother held a fistful of diamonds.

"These are almost too precious to turn into jewelry," her mother continued as she heaped diamonds, sapphires, and rubies onto the table.

"We should keep some of them," Lavinia said. "We—"

Her mother's frown stopped Lavinia from speaking further. However, when her mother turned and looked deeper into the sack, Lavinia quickly pocketed two diamonds for herself.

LAVINIA and her mother fashioned what gems they could into jewelry, then offered the rest for sale. Patrons at the market began to swarm their table. Lavinia was grateful for the crowds, not only for their patronage, but because they could distract her mother while she pocketed a few coins before she added them to the till.

Lavinia kept the two diamonds and her increasing coins under her pillow. Each night, she felt their ridges and points against her cheeks and she smiled, dreaming sweet dreams of the wealth she'd amass. Soon she'd leave the cottage in the woods. She'd use the money to buy dresses and jewelry, perhaps to buy her way into a marriage with a wealthy widower. Let her mother and Penelope fend for themselves in this joke of a home. Let Penelope spend her afternoons digging for rocks once she was old enough. Lavinia was ready for more.

THEIR TREASURE TROVE SOON DEPLETED. Lavinia collected lesser crystals from the woods, but they didn't sell as well as the finer jewelry she and her mother had been selling lately. "Once folks see a diamond, they'll never settle for another gem," her mother sighed as they walked home from a lackluster day at the market.

Lavinia didn't answer. She thought instead of the two diamonds under her pillow. Perhaps if she and her mother kept the diamonds scarce at their table, she could sell them for an even higher sum when her mother wasn't looking. Then she could run away with her riches.

The next morning, her mother dropped the burlap sack at Lavinia's feet while she broke her fast. "Go back to your mine this morning," her mother instructed.

Lavinia stopped eating and shivered at the memory of the tendrils tightening over her skin. "Surely people can do with quartz," she said.

"Did you take all the diamonds and sapphires from the cave before?"

"No, but they're hard to come by."

"Customers are hard to come by. Bring us something good. It's what our buyers want."

Lavinia continued eating in silence. She knew better than to contradict her mother. However, she wouldn't be coming back with a sack full of diamonds. She'd carry just enough to add to the riches she'd placed under her pillow. It was time to leave. Before picking up the sack, she pocketed her butter knife. This time, she'd be prepared for the cave.

IT SEEMED Lavinia walked for ages before the familiar glimmer caught her eye. She turned and saw the cave through a clearing. Its opening was dark and empty. No stones lay in sight at the cave's mouth. Lavinia sighed, then moved forward. She rubbed the handle of her butter knife like a worry stone to give her courage.

She'd barely stepped both feet inside before the light snuffed out. Lavinia didn't tremble. She was used to this by now, and also used to the faint whisper that spoke as if it were a passing thought: "What do you want?"

"You know what I want," Lavinia answered.

A sigh rang in her ears. The cave's floor pulsed beneath her feet. Lavinia shivered as she felt it warm up and breathe, as if she were standing on a monster's chest.

"And you know what I want," the whisper replied.

Lavinia didn't speak. Instead, she removed the butter knife and pressed the sharper end into her palm. It took a few tries, but at last, blood began to seep from the scratch. She knelt and placed her bleeding hand upon the cave floor.

The breathing stopped. The rock became cool to her touch. Lavinia waited for the darkness to disappear and for mountains of stones to appear for the taking.

"I already have this blood," the whisper hissed.

Lavinia furrowed her brow. "What more could you want?"

"More."

"You have more." Lavinia rubbed her hand more furiously across the ground.

"More sources."

"Sources?"

The darkness disappeared. A beam of sun from outside came so sharply that Lavinia nearly doubled back from its brightness. The cave floor was bare.

Lavinia screamed in anger. The whisper didn't reply. She only heard the echo of her anger and a distant bird chirping in the trees. Lavinia held the knife, then began to stab the cave's walls. Tiny chunks of rock fell to the ground. She worked until a small hill formed at her feet. She'd come for stones, and she'd be damned if she left without any.

HER MOTHER FROWNED when Lavinia entered the cottage. "Less gems today?" she asked as she set Penelope back in her crib.

"Better than nothing," Lavinia replied as she set the bag on the table. She furrowed her brow at the lack of sound the stones made. Before she could investigate, her mother peered inside the bag. Her mother's mouth dropped and her eyes widened in anger.

"What did you bring back?" she asked as she reached inside.

"Are the stones gone?"

"There are no stones, just ash!" Her mother lifted up her hand and let a river of ash fall back into the bag.

Tears pricked Lavinia's eyes. She bit her lip to keep from cursing.

Her mother softened. "Look, it's alright—we've made so much the past few weeks from the diamonds and sapphires you found. We can last on that for a while longer—"

"It's not enough," Lavinia spat.

"We have enough."

"We never do! We only have enough for you and your wants!" Lavinia grabbed the bag and hurled it across the room. "You are happy in this cottage! You are happy with plain clothes and just enough for food and drink!"

"Don't speak to me that way!"

"You are happy giving everything we have to this squalor in the forest, these customers who get everything we make, that baby who eats and shits through all we have—"

Her mother slapped Lavinia across the face. "How dare you speak of your sister that way! Our home! How did I raise such a spoiled, ungrateful brat?"

"I hate it here! I hate our scarcity and I hate not having anything I WANT!" Lavinia stormed into her room and slammed it shut. She pulled a trunk in front of the door so her mother couldn't come in. Knocks sounded as Lavinia scrambled to her bed.

"Lavinia! Open the door!"

Lavinia ignored her mother and reached for her pillow. She'd take her riches and leave right then and there.

The pillow felt light in her hands. Lavinia paled. "No, no, no ..." she whispered as she turned the pillow over. Ash fell from inside the pillowcase. "NO!"

"LAVINIA!"

Lavinia fell to the bed, sobbing. The cave wanted more. Lavinia had given her fear, her time, even her blood; but the cave wouldn't take it. It only wanted more—and now, it had taken away what little it had given. Lavinia cried harder as her mother continued slamming against the door.

The door finally heaved against the trunk enough to provide a gap. Her mother barged in and lifted Lavinia by the wrist to her feet. "I don't know what's possessed you, child," her mother hissed. "But you'll stop that crying right this instant!"

"Leave me alone!"

Her mother slapped her again. Lavinia hung her head and continued to weep. As her sobbing quieted, she heard Penelope begin to shriek from the other room. That cursed baby. She wasn't good for anything.

"Oh for goodness sake," her mother said as she let Lavinia go. "Look what you've done to your sister. She'll scream until she bleeds if you don't quiet down.

Lavinia sniffed and stared as her mother went into the other room. She watched as her mother lifted Penelope, who screamed and wailed over her mother's shoulder. Penelope's face was flushed crimson. Lavinia could almost feel her sister's pulse within her own.

She knew what she had to do.

Lavinia waited until her mother was asleep before creeping towards Penelope's crib. She lifted her sister carefully so as not to wake her. Penelope stirred and began to suck her thumb, but didn't cry. Her mother let out a loud snore and turned away from both of them. Lavinia gently wrapped her sister in her sack, then held her close as she tiptoed out of the cottage.

As she walked into the woods with nothing but the full moon to light her way, she thought of stories she could tell when her mother woke up and found Penelope missing. A thief had entered the cottage, and Lavinia only woke up when he'd slammed the door behind him, baby in hand. Or perhaps a wolf, one that Lavinia couldn't stop no matter how quickly she'd run after it. Maybe she'd say nothing at all. Penelope was learning to crawl. Would her mother believe that she'd gotten out of the crib herself and wandered into the forest?

The forest grew darker with every step Lavinia took. Lavinia thought of the ashes beneath her pillow, and how her chance to run away had been lost. She held Penelope tighter. Not this time. In fact, why even return home at all? Soon the sack wrapped around her sister would be filled with riches. She'd ask no more from the cave, and the cave would have nothing to take away from her. She'd run away, use her riches to get far and to get all the things she wanted. Let her mother live alone and rot outside of the woods with her cords and her gems. Lavinia had bigger plans.

The all-too familiar glint caught Lavinia's eye. She turned and saw the cave beneath the moonlight. Unlike its appearance during the day, a faint orange glow emanated from within the opening. Lavinia smiled, grateful she wouldn't be plunged into darkness this time. Hopefully the rest of the cave would be better behaved than the last time.

Penelope squirmed and let out a small, single cry. "And you behave too," Lavinia said in a hushed voice as she walked towards the cave.

Lavinia stepped across the threshold and heard the same sigh she'd heard so many times. She still shuddered at the sound of it all the same.

"What do you want?" the whisper asked.

Lavinia swallowed and straightened her posture. In doing so, she caught a quick glance to her side. She paused and widened her eyes. The entrance was gone, and now, in the soft orange glow, she saw nothing but the cave's walls. They were orange and pink beneath the light—discerningly like flesh.

"What do you want?" the whisper repeated.

Lavinia collected herself. "I want to give you what you want," she replied. She unraveled Penelope from the sack.

"I've no use for a baby."

"You wanted blood that wasn't mine."

"Babies have no wants. Only needs."

Lavinia's face grew warm. Penelope began to squirm and wriggle in Lavinia's arms. "You said you needed more sources of blood! Does a baby not have blood?"

"You stole from my body."

"What?"

"The stones you chipped."

"Those stones turned to ash!"

"My body is precious. The price is to receive my gifts. To keep them is higher."

"How could it go any higher?" Lavinia yelled. Penelope shrieked in response and began to cry. She thrashed against Lavinia's breast in search of comforting milk, butting her head over and over as she wailed. Lavinia put her down and hissed, "Shut up, you beast!"

Penelope rolled onto her hands and feet and began to crawl away. Lavinia watched in horror as a tiny opening appeared where there had been walls, small enough for Penelope to escape.

"No!" Lavinia cried. She only managed one step forward, though, before a familiar tendril grasped her ankle. "Let me go!"

But it was too late. Penelope reached the exit and vanished. The gap closed behind her, taking away Lavinia's one path back to the forest.

"The forest will see her home," the whisper said.

"Let me go!" Lavinia cried again. Tendrils grabbed her other ankle, then both wrists. "You said you didn't need me."

"I didn't need you for trade." The tendrils began to curl around Lavinia slowly, almost seductively, as if they were a lover. "But you, my dear, are filled with wanting. Wanting that will never vanish."

"All I want is to get out!" Lavinia thrashed against the tendrils. The cave plunged into darkness. A single glimmer sparkled in the black surrounding her.

Lavinia stilled. One glimmer became two. Two became four. Four became twenty. Soon she was surrounded by sparkles, diamonds that glimmered without light, stones that begged to be touched but could never be reached.

"They thought that was all they wanted, too," the whisper said.

The glimmering began to fade. In place of the sparkles, Lavinia saw white, wet spots. They flickered in and out of blackness. Orbs of brown, white, green, and blue. A thousand pairs of eyes surrounded her, blinking and dripping tears onto her hair.

Lavinia screamed, her wail bouncing off the walls she couldn't see, walls hidden behind curtains of eyes that billowed around her. The whisper sounded over her cries: "But it wasn't all they wanted. They were forever filled with want, a greed that could never be quenched."

Lavinia resumed her thrashing and screaming. "Let me go! Help! Help me!" She tried to pull her wrist towards her mouth so she could gnaw at the tendril. The tendril slammed back her wrist with such force that she felt a bone break against the cave's wall. She cried out in pain, then in shock when she realized she felt something cold and smooth against her toes.

"I cannot be quenched either," the whisper said.

The cold, smooth wall pressed closer against her feet, then against both sides of her body. Tears streamed down Lavinia's cheeks. "No, no—"

"But humans are so much easier to come by than stones."

The walls squeezed Lavinia from both sides. She cried out one last time before she felt every piece of her crush between the walls. The last thing she saw was a tiny glimmer where her fingertips once were.

"It's time to collect stones today."

Penelope smiled as she took the sack from her mother. Overall, she loved collecting gems for her mother to fashion into jewelry. But as she approached her twelfth birthday, she started to wonder if she really needed to be spending so much time collecting stones.

She didn't dare ask her mother—the one time she dared mention it, her mother grew cross and warned her not to become like the older sister she'd never met, who grew ungrateful and ran away.

Penelope wouldn't dream of leaving. She loved their humble cottage, their proximity to a beautiful forest, and her mother, whose jewelry seemed otherworldly in its beauty. Penelope looked at the trees and sighed before stooping to search for gems. But sometimes, she wondered: what if there could be more?

A small glimmer caught Penelope's attention. She looked towards it and saw a cave she'd never seen before. One glimmer, then two, shone from its mouth.

Penelope smiled and walked towards the cave. Maybe, perhaps, something a little more wouldn't be so bad.

ABOUT THE EDITOR / PUBLISHER

Dawn Shea is an author and half of the publishing team over at D&T Publishing. She lives with her family in Mississippi. Always an avid horror lover, she has moved forward with her dreams of writing and publishing those things she loves so much.

D&T Previously published material:

ABC's of Terror

After the Kool-Aid is Gone

Follow her author page on Amazon for all publications she is featured in.

Follow D&T Publishing at the following locations:

Website

Facebook: Page / Group

Or email us here: dandtpublishing20@gmail.com

The Avarice - A Seven Deadly Sins Anthology

Edited by Dawn Shea

Cover by Don Noble

Formatting by J.Z. Foster

Corinth, MS

www.ingramcontent.com/pod-product-compliance
Lightning Source LLC
LaVergne TN
LVHW041101150826
845673LV00007B/1874

* 9 7 9 8 8 4 8 3 7 2 3 6 6 *